(IN)VISIBLE

GUERNICA WORLD EDITIONS 71

(IN)VISIBLE

IVAN BAIDAK

Translated from the Ukrainian
by Hanna Leliv and Isaac Wheeler

GUERNICA
World
EDITIONS

TORONTO—CHICAGO—BUFFALO—LANCASTER (U.K.)
2022

Original title: *(Не)помітні* (2020)
Ukrainian copyright © 2020, Vivat Publishing
Translation copyright © 2022, Hanna Leliv, Isaac Wheeler
and Guernica Editions Inc.

Guernica Editions Founder: Antonio D'Alfonso

Michael Mirolla, general editor
Anna van Valkenburg, editor
Interior design: Jill Ronsley, suneditwrite.com
Cover design: Allen Jomoc Jr.
Cover image: Lesya Yasnitska

Guernica Editions Inc.
287 Templemead Drive, Hamilton (ON), Canada L8W 2W4
2250 Military Road, Tonawanda, N.Y. 14150-6000 U.S.A.
www.guernicaeditions.com

Distributors:
Independent Publishers Group (IPG)
600 North Pulaski Road, Chicago IL 60624
University of Toronto Press Distribution (UTP)
5201 Dufferin Street, Toronto (ON), Canada M3H 5T8
Gazelle Book Services, White Cross Mills
High Town, Lancaster LA1 4XS U.K.

First edition.
Printed in Canada.

Legal Deposit—Third Quarter
Library of Congress Catalog Card Number: 2022940815
Library and Archives Canada Cataloguing in Publication
Title: (In)visible / Ivan Baidak ; translated from the Ukrainian by Hanna
Leliv and Isaac Wheeler.
Names: Baidak, Ivan, author. | Leliv, Hanna, translator. | Wheeler, Isaac
Stackhouse, translator.
Series: Guernica world editions ; 71.
Description: Series statement: Guernica world editions ; 71
Identifiers: Canadiana (print) 20220265291 | Canadiana (ebook)
2022027102X | ISBN 9781771838528
(softcover) | ISBN 9781771838535 (EPUB)
Classification: LCC PG3950.12.A534 H3713 2022 | DDC 891.7/934—dc23

To my sister
who knows me better than I do.

Our family always had dinner in silence. My father would return home irritable after an exhausting shift at the factory, and he couldn't bear our chatter. Mama knew his habits all too well, and she could tell whenever he wanted a second helping, a pinch of salt, or another beer. I was expected to finish my meal as quickly as possible and make myself scarce. I liked it better when my father had night shifts. Then Mama and I could joke and laugh a lot. It's not that I didn't love my father—I just felt more comfortable having dinner when I wasn't worrying that I might drop a knife on the floor or stain the tablecloth.

That night, Father came home wiped. He drank more than usual and vented to Mama about his boss, and then he started grilling me about things at school and the sports club. Once he'd heard what he wanted, he reached for another beer.

"Stop blinking!" Father burst out, glaring at me.

I froze. Then I grew agitated and started blinking even harder.

"Didn't you two go to the doctor last month?" he asked Mama.

"Yes, but he said that tics aren't easily cured."

"Then find another doctor who can sort him out! Last thing I need is people thinking that my son is dumb."

Mama was angry, but she kept quiet. I couldn't hold back my tics.

"It's been years now," Father said. "Can't they give you pills or something? I'm working my ass off to support this family, and what do I get for it? A damn disgrace! What are you going to do with him anyway? He'll need to get a job one day."

Father glared at me.

"Stop that at once!" he yelled, but I just couldn't stop twitching. "Can't you hear?"

7

"Enough!" Mama said. "He can't help it, as you well know."
Father stopped yelling, and muttered:
"Then he'll have to learn to control it."

———•———

It's been a while, but I still remember that episode. I honestly couldn't understand what Father was demanding of me that night, but I didn't want to wind him up even more, so I tried to make my body listen to me. Later, my whole life would be centered around controlling my tics so that people wouldn't see me as "different," and I wouldn't have to explain "what was wrong with me" all the time. I heard these two phrases more often than any others. At some point, I caught myself thinking that my tics were taking over my entire life—I had to secure their approval for all my actions and plans. It sometimes felt like friendship. How ironic. It was nothing but madness.

I'm tired of it. I came here to break free.
"Hello. I'm Adam. I'm a graphic designer. Freelance. I love watching TV series, and I hate shopping. I'm 26. I have Tourette's syndrome."

———•———

Hello. I'm Ivan. I am a writer. I love helping people, and I hate discrimination. I started writing this novel when I was 29. I have Tourette's syndrome.

I first realized that I was "different" when a university professor asked me to leave the room because my sniffing made it hard for her to read her lecture. All my life, I've been struggling with the side effects of Tourette's syndrome. I was fired from jobs; my girlfriends broke up with me; passers-by mimicked my movements just for fun. Had I written this book a few years ago, it would have been full of memories like that, negative emotions, and reflections about the unfairness of the world—which is a confirmed fact, by the way. It's just that each of us has their personal reason for saying that. This book, though, is not about negative things. Neither is it a bold coming-out. It is a silent coming to terms with my own lived experience. It is a call to not give up on yourself. It is a plea for acceptance of others.

A disclaimer. Adam's story is not the story of my own life, and there's no point in looking for similarities. Even so, let me assure you: there's a lot of truth in it.

ADAM

"HELLO, ADAM," said a short middle-aged man.
"Hello, Adam," repeated everyone else in unison.

It was a social support group for people with challenges. My
therapist recommended that I join it. Sitting in a circle, people took
turns to tell their stories, share their feelings, and listen to the words
of understanding and support from others like them. It took me a
whole month to work up the courage to tell my story. Until then,
I'd been only listening to others as if I'd wanted to make sure that it
was safe. On the one hand, that therapy method offered some comfort, but on the other, human stories were usually too emotional,
and that's what made them destructive—you could relate to any of
them, and it ripped open your old wounds. My tic was noticeable,
to be sure, but they ignored it just like they ignored the challenges
of other group members.

At my first meeting, I couldn't handle more than fifteen minutes. Memories came flooding back, and I jumped to my feet and
dashed for the door, interrupting someone's story.

"You're leaving already?" a girl asked, stopping me halfway. She
had a big lump that looked like a ball of skin on her cheek.

"Yeah ... I live on the other side of town. Don't want to miss
the last bus."

"So, you live across the bridge?" she asked.

I nodded.

"I can give you a lift. It's on my way."

I said thank you and took my seat again, but I tried to tune out everything that was happening around me. I should've thanked her and turned her offer down, of course. She could obviously see that I had no trouble getting back home. But it turned out for the better that I stayed.

That was how I met my first friend with challenges. Actually, Anna became my first ever friend. I kept people at a distance unless circumstances forced them to talk to me. Sooner or later, any new connection reached the point when I had to explain why I was having the tics, which wasn't my favourite thing to do. Just imagine that you have to explain—to justify—why you're 5'11" tall, or why you have black hair, brown eyes, and a mole near your left eye.

I had to do that for my Tourette's syndrome all the time, and it damaged my relationships irreparably—no matter the sincere sympathy, get-well wishes, or even doctors' recommendations.

I didn't have to explain anything to Anna. But I wanted to because she could hear me out. She could really understand me.

Anna had a hemangioma—a benign tumor on her cheek. She couldn't have it removed because a carotid artery ran right through it.

"I get emails from doctors across the world. They all offer their help. A few professors even flew in to see me. But MRI scans left no chance for surgery. A while ago, I still had hope. I believed. I was looking at different options. But now I know the mystical healing scenario all too well. And I'm no longer bothered."

"And how are you doing, in general, these days?" I asked, trying to change the subject. I had enough stories at the support group meeting that night.

"How am I doing? Great. I spend most of my days working. Making clothes. My co-workers are nice, and I like my job. I could do more, to be sure, and one day things will change. It's just that some people are assholes, and they don't see me as I am ... you know why ..."

I nodded.

"I even got myself a car to avoid public transport. Whenever I took a subway, someone would always kill my mood with their stares."

"I know," I said, unable to squeeze out more than two words.

"But it's okay. You know it, right? It's just a matter of choice of how you decide to feel about it: angry, hurt, hateful, ironic ... I go for this last one. Sometimes, I can even make fun of myself. I often say that I'm going to remodel my face just like I remodel clothes. Not the best joke, I know."

"I live around the corner from here," I said. The joke was not funny at all.

"Well, this is quite far out, buddy."

"I'm trying to save up money to move out of my parents' house," I said.

"Move in with me, if you like," she said.

I merely smiled.

"No! I'm serious. Girls and I are renting a three-bedroom apartment. One of my flatmates has just moved out. So, one room for me, one for Marta—I met her at a support group meeting, too. And there's another spare room. Pack up and give it a go if you want to. Just let me know by next Thursday."

Smiling again, I got out of the car.

———•·•———

By the way, my father apologized for that dinner incident, and I promised I'd try not to twitch, as if that was something I enjoyed. Tics are sudden uncontrollable movements of muscles in different parts of the body. Suppose you want to raise your hand—your brain sends a nerve impulse to your hand, telling it to do it. With tics, these impulses are not controlled. That's a very brief explanation of

Tourette's syndrome. I make no claims to medical accuracy, to be sure, but that's how I made sense of my illness after many attempts to treat it.

I'm still trying not to bother people around me. I go shopping when there aren't too many customers at the store, and I prefer supermarkets and self-service stations to avoid too much attention. I told the cashier at a neighbourhood grocery about my illness, so she never asks unwelcome questions. To tell the truth, I feel relieved when I tell others about my condition, even though I don't like talking about it.

I hide in my hoodie on public transport, skip all kinds of exciting meetings and events, and don't let myself go to the movies or other public places so as not to bother other people. I even avoid sitting by a café window during lunch, just in case my tics scare the potential customers away. When tourists ask me for help, I usually say no to avoid contact or uncomfortable situations, although I do have some qualms about it.

I've thought up excuses for all kinds of questions:

"I caught a cold," I say when I'm struggling with sniffing;

"I have a stiff neck," I say when my head suddenly jerks.

In some situations, these explanations help.

I never went to college. After I finished school, my father got me a job at the nail factory where he was working. I held out for only two weeks. I got a deep gash to my hand when the tics defeated me, so I had to look for another, safer job. I spent some time sorting mail at the post office, but I wanted to work with people, so I decided to become a sales rep. Over a year, I had fifty job interviews with wine merchants, sweet shops, and bakeries, travel agencies, language schools, and internet providers. None of them turned me down—they just kept silent. Only at one interview did I hear what was probably the truth at least half the time.

"You'll have to work with other people, you know. Your movements ... they create certain distrust. This job involves a lot of communication. The person doing it will be the company's public face. Our clients might have a mixed reaction, I'm afraid."

My job search ended right there. Or wait—there was another story. I somehow managed to control my tics during an interview, only to be fired on my third day at work.

"Unconvincing sales strategies," they said.

My prospects were unconvincing, too, but I moved on to become a graphic designer.

I ran into my art teacher in the street. She'd always been incredibly kind to me—because of my tics, perhaps, or simply because I liked painting. She told me about her son who worked as a designer and recommended that I give it a try.

I did. And things went well. After an online course in graphic design, after thousands of minutes of videos and as many hours of practice, I signed up on a freelance website and found my first client. He then recommended me to his friend who owned an advertising agency. That's how I landed a full-time job.

Now I'm a designer with three years' experience. I work from home, never meet my clients in person, and sometimes Skype with my workmates. With my camera off. Twice a week, I go grocery shopping. In the evenings, I watch TV series. I don't talk to my neighbours; I don't use social media; I don't have friends. That's what my life is like. I work as a designer, and I try not to bother other people. And I'm fine with it. I've created a routine that I enjoy. Some time ago, Mama started to worry about my mental health. A therapist visited me for a while. That's when I joined the social support group.

My parents. I'm still living with them. But our relationship broke down a long time ago. Mama often seems to be eager to leave me be. But in fact, I'm pushing her away by feeling indifferent to my own life. My father … I don't think that he's ever wanted to fix his relationship with me. After that incident at the nail factory, he made another attempt—he tried to teach me to drive. But during the very first tic attack, I lost control and ran into another car in front of me. That was it for my driving lessons. And not only for them.

The next week, I moved to Anna's place.

I feel that otherness is inside us—in what we think about, in what we consider important, in how we treat people around us. It has always surprised me how different we can be; how different people are interested in different things, from drama to machine-building; how they have different tastes in music and food; how they root for different sports teams. Our appearance can be part of what others like about us, but can it become an object of ridicule, mockery, or discrimination?

Our society has learned to accept people with disabilities even though it can't always provide the conditions they need. Scared of the words "cancer" and "AIDS," we've developed an empathetic form of response to them. Low-income groups get all kinds of help. We've been fighting hard against gender and racial inequality. Yet, people with disfigurements are left outside this system of acceptance.

One day, on my way back home, I met a man with Tourette's syndrome on the tram. I remember him taking a back seat—to avoid unwanted attention, most probably. His head jerked. He made some random sounds, and I saw he was trying to control himself. When passengers started to make disapproving noises, his body tensed up, and his tic worsened, so I went closer and, stopping in front of him so he could see my blinking, I tried to make him understand: he was not alone. He took the hint and smiled. His tic attack calmed.

How to respond is always a delicate question. It's never clear what is the right way to react: to look away—or to let your eyes linger. Either reaction might hurt the person. There was another situation: I saw a girl with Tourette's syndrome on the bus, but when she noticed my tics, she burst out screaming and crying, and then she hurled insults at me. At the next stop, the girl got off in a fit of tears, and I followed her, trying to excuse myself and explain that I was just like her.

"I'm just like you," I said, trying to calm her down. "I have tics, too. I didn't do that on purpose."

She slapped me. All I remember is her flushed, tear-stained face. Did she hurt my feelings? No, she didn't.

Back in the days when I was still struggling to work at the factory, one of my co-workers tried to copy my tics. It was just a joke for him. He didn't do it out of spite, I realize now, but at that moment, I felt like grabbing a tool and killing him. Could that girl really believe that I had the same rare disorder like her? Hardly. That's why I held no grudge against her. That co-worker of mine also remained unhurt, even though I had to describe to him in graphic detail what kind of accidents could happen on the production floor.

Whenever I meet someone with a disorder, it helps me accept myself and understand other people whose attention—just like mine—is drawn to everything unusual. This seems to be human nature: unusual things attract us, and we're wired to react. We should be aware enough, though, to react appropriately—that's what matters.

———·•·———

How can you explain your disorder to others?

This was the subject of our next group meeting. At these get-togethers, we usually talked about living with challenges, and we listened to people who needed to get it off their chests.

"There's no way I can do it," Anna, the first to speak, said. "I just say that I have a hemangioma and let them wonder what that is. Otherwise, I'd spend all day re-telling the history of my disorder to the curious. But then, perhaps, I should charge for that. That would be a nice way to make some cash and entertain people at the same time."

"How can you explain your challenge to others, and do you have to do it at all?" David, our group therapist, asked, stepping in. "It's not a good idea to dwell on uncomfortable things or situations if you can help it. When we're talking to others, our explanations sometimes sound like justifications. But everyone seeks approval one way or another. Especially from the person they're in a relationship with. And it doesn't matter if that person has a challenge. We want them to approve our hard work, our opinions, our funny jokes. That's why you should talk about your challenge to the people you're working, socializing, or building relationships with. It will put you at ease, both of you, because that person—believe me—also feels discomfort, as they're not sure if their behaviour hurts you."

"But what about random people?" someone asked.

"You can tell them all about it, ignore them, or just say that it's an intolerant question, you're not comfortable answering it, and could they stop bothering you," David said. "Do what's comfortable for you."

"But some people can react badly to that."

"Right. But you must learn how to stand up for yourself."

"I usually joke about it," Eva said. "Whenever someone asks me about the patches on my skin, I pretend I have no idea what they're talking about. 'Patches? What patches? What's wrong with me? Perhaps, there's something wrong with you? It's all your imagination. I don't have any patches. Are you feeling unwell? Should I call a doctor? It's so hot today.' This is my way of dealing with it, and it's very effective and fun."

"And how would you like others to treat you?" David asked.

"I wish they didn't notice us at all," Anna said. "Or, rather, ignored us. Well … people can get sensitive even about someone's bright hair colour or unconventional clothes. But I would still like to attract less attention. And it doesn't really matter whether it's negative or positive. I don't care. Once, I volunteered to help a girl in a wheelchair to get to a concert. It was a large stadium, big crowds, so we took a taxi home instead of a bus. I remember how the driver stared at us in the mirror, and when we arrived, he refused to take our money. An act of kindness, alright, but it hurt my feelings. I don't want anyone's help when I'm not asking for it."

The meeting finished, as always, with a heated discussion. People shared their thoughts, healing their wounds.

"I'll be happy if today's conversation helps you better under-stand yourselves," David said, wrapping it up. "Please remember that you're just like any other people, and you also have the right to a decent life and relationships. Don't be so hard on others. They might just need a bit more time to get used to you, but there's noth-ing bad about that."

Then everyone left. But I remember that David's last phrase ruffled Eva's feelings.

"What's the matter?" I asked, seeing her looking annoyed.

"Did you hear what he said? They just need 'to get used' to us, but it 'doesn't mean anything'! No, Adam, it means a lot. It means that people will always have 'to get used' to me, learn to accept me, and understand me. It means that, whenever I meet someone, I have to spend the first ten minutes assuring them that I'm normal. It means that I always have to create a bubble around me. It means that I can never make a good first impression—it's always a bit weird—and that no one will fall in love with me at first sight. It means a lot more than that, Adam."

———•·•———

I have got used to living with tics. But I will hardly ever get used to its surprising new forms, just like I will never make peace with the fact that I have to live through this. I have long been trying to understand my feelings, but I could never put my finger on the format of our relationship. I'm in a constant struggle with my body. Each of its new tricks catches me unawares. My body can make me cough, jerk my neck, blink, raise my hands, stretch my legs, shout out random sounds. It looks like some kind of a role play for dom-ination, but I often get tired of the battle which feels more like a game of anti-chess.

I might find myself buttoning my shirt up and down dozens of times, winding my watch, playing with my phone, opening and closing popular apps as if performing some ritual. I don't always tie my shoes because I get angry when I can't align the eyelets. I have to be extra careful when cooking. There's always a risk I might burn myself. I steer clear of amusement parks because it might have a sad ending. I'm afraid of having sex, too, since I'm not sure I'll be able to control the moment of orgasm. That's very distressing.

Sometimes, I want to hurt myself, to punish this body of mine that gets so tired of itself that it keeps aching and causing muscle cramps. If you don't sleep well, your tic is sure to exhaust you in the morning. If you let yourself drink more coffee or alcohol than usual, it will destroy you. Even if I won a million dollars in the lottery, the joy I'd feel would only make my tic worse. That's why I avoid all kinds of emotional triggers: I don't read bad news; I don't watch dramas; I protect myself from intense emotions. It's quite uncomfortable. A life like this is not fun. I wish I could make a bargain with Tourette's syndrome or, at least, take a brief vacation from it.

———•·•———

It was curious that the reactions we discussed at the most recent group meeting depended on a person's age. Seniors were the most annoying—well-versed in pretty much everything, they knew the solutions to all my problems. One woman, an ardent believer, nearly dragged me to a church where they had an icon of some saint on display. That category of people was the most troublesome because they tried too hard to help, to the point of being intrusive. Teenagers shouted insults or made rude gestures, but that also didn't hurt, since they didn't fully understand their actions. The reaction of my peers, young men and women, was the weakest. They usually pretended not to notice anything and played it by ear, feigning indifference, compassion, or understanding. That was the worst. In the rare moments when they did notice me, like in a café, their wordless glances and barely audible whispers always spoke the loudest.

———•·•———

The new routine swallowed me whole. Now, the three of us—Anna, Marta, and I—lived together. I continued to work from home. Anna returned after the morning shift around noon. Marta's schedule remained unclear. She often locked herself in her room. Marta and I didn't talk much. Each of us had a separate bedroom, and in the evenings, we got together in a large living room to discuss the events of the day or share memories. Eva lived in our neighbourhood, and she often dropped in. We created our own social mini-group.

My reclusive life—working from home, giving Mama some money for groceries, rarely going outside, seeing only a small circle of friends—started to change. The new circumstances were not quite comfortable, as all things new scared me, but I definitely benefitted from them. I had some new household chores, like paying the utility bills. It was stressful, too: I was worried that the post office employees would think there was something wrong with me and call the police … or an ambulance. Anna invited her friends over sometimes and urged me to join her volunteer projects. Finding myself in unfamiliar situations, I built up my confidence. It took me a long while to regain it, though. We were young and carefree once, and we entered adult life with confidence and optimism, but it was amazing how quickly the world put us in our place—and how long it took to recover that positive attitude. Just a short time ago, I had been looking for a job that required lots of communication. I had often smiled, and I could not even imagine that the tic would become such a huge problem.

I had long since forgotten the meaning of friendship. It seemed to be something that had existed only in childhood. But now the four of us cooked dinner together, watched movies, and discussed all kinds of issues—from Latin American literature to how automation would replace the human workforce—devising a few schemes for fighting plastic waste along the way. We chuckled and giggled, and burst into song like drunks whenever Eva brought her guitar. No matter how awful things had been "outside," inside, all of us felt at ease. It felt good to be together, and we needed each other.

"I have never ridden a bicycle in my life," Marta said.

"And I have never smoked," Anna said. "It would be too dangerous for me," she added, explaining herself for some reason.

We were playing *Never Have I Ever*. I remembered so many things I had never tried, or rather, I had never allowed myself to try. Ceramics had always fascinated me. I wanted to try to make something out of clay, but I didn't want my tic to bother anyone, and I wasn't sure I could control myself long enough to finish my work.

The conversation lasted deep into the night. We shared our dreams and made our bucket lists. It felt as if all of it would finally come true. A new stage in our lives had begun. Feeling safe, we looked boldly to the future, disregarding the dark past.

The following week, my flatmates and I attended Eva's exhibition. Eva had talked about it for a long while. But she had worried about public reaction so much that she'd nearly cancelled it on several occasions.

"You're almost there. Don't back out now," Anna told her, trying to calm her nerves.

It was an exhibition of Eva's nude photos. She decided to undress and show the public what vitiligo looked like. In a long narrow hallway, twenty photographs of naked Eva hung, showing her body from different angles. I wondered whether the connoisseurs of that photography style appreciated the photos. But it was most curious to watch the public react to vitiligo.

"My wife's put on a lot of weight lately," a man in his forties said, "but this looks even worse."

His was the only negative comment for the entire opening night, though.

People arrived and looked at the pieces in silence or whispered a few words to each other, pretending they understood the key message of the exhibition. After all, that was exactly what you were expected to do when you didn't understand something. A random visitor might have thought that it was an exhibition of birth defects or a dermatology conference. There was a small reception afterwards, though, and the atmosphere livened up. The guests enjoyed their drinks and had fun, forgetting that they had came there to discuss equality for people with appearance issues. But then, people do joke at funerals, claiming that the deceased was high-spirited and that's exactly the farewell they would have wanted.

The exhibition was followed by a brief press conference where Eva spoke about the history of her illness, treatments, public moods, and the idea behind her project.

"What are people most curious about in your case?" a woman asked during the Q&A session.

"They wonder if my illness is infectious," Eva said, smiling. "Most often, I get this question from people sitting next to me on the train or an airplane."

"Does your vitiligo limit you in any way?"

"I used to have a handful of limitations. But now only one is left. I take care in the sun and cover up when it gets too hot. When I was little, I got a sunburn during a sporting event and developed blisters all over the discoloured areas of my skin. They hurt for a month or so. That was when I realized I'd better avoid the sun when it's really scorching out. That is my only limitation."

"What are your biggest fears?"

"I was scared that people would not accept me. I was afraid of insults. Negative stuff is uncomfortable for anyone, after all. But I was anxious that my work, my ideas, my thoughts would not be accepted, just because of my appearance. That is a thing of the past, though. I have already passed that stage."

"So, you don't have any fears now?"

"I'm only afraid that my children will get vitiligo. But as far as I am concerned, no, I don't have any fears."

"What is the message of your exhibition?" a reporter asked. "And how should people react to appearance issues?"

"They should know that these things exist and that many people around them are different. But I wish they would not react to it at all."

This was the last question. Informal conversations resumed. People walked around the exhibition, taking pictures with their phones, or simple came up and thanked our friend Eva—Eva who had made it as a makeup artist and finally achieved emotional closure.

EVA

I WOKE UP and first saw my mother. She was sitting on a chair next to my bed, napping, until her eyes and mine opened at the same time.

"Now that's a strong maternal instinct," a voice in my head said. Another voice added, with reproach, that I'd neglected the role of a good daughter. Mama looked anxious. She had never been able to control her emotions, so I knew there was a problem (and not only with Mama). I started to speak really fast, trying to explain myself, but the words wouldn't come out. The problem was clearly serious. I made another unsuccessful attempt, and then I looked at Mama questioningly: "What's wrong with me?" She fell back helplessly into her chair. It was a verdict. I wept for a long time. Weeping was the only skill my body was still capable of. Mama was gazing at my intensely, and the last thing I thought before I went back to sleep was that she forgave me, even though she did not understand me.

———•———

When I was a little girl, *Terminator* became my first grown-up movie. I liked Arnie's strength and unusual appearance, and I dreamed that one day I would get metal plates in my own body, too. I thought that it would give me plenty of dividends, but all I got in real life was learning to walk over again, using my hands properly, and maneuvering around carefully, without jerking. My rehabilitation took almost a year. I followed a set schedule, eating healthy food, getting enough sleep, reading books on my TBR list, and limiting my communication to doctors at the hospital—fortunately, the condition of my bones interested them much more than my vitiligo.

Later, I very much ~~regretted~~ raged about what had happened to me. Throughout my eventful history of hospital stays, I noticed a curious category of patients—the healthy. Those people grew so weary of living that an in-patient department looked like a pretext for a well-earned rest. At some point, I admitted that it was quite comfortable to play the victim and feel sorry for yourself—it was easier that way. I promised myself that I would never ever allow myself to do it.

———— · • · ————

You do not want to do this. Just like I did not. I never searched for a bridge high enough so the jump would not leave me any chance of survival. I never researched substances that could cause organ dysfunction and the death of my body. I never pondered what kind of suicide would be the least painful for me or most shocking for others. I had no intention of masking the suicide as an accident. I did not write any explanatory notes or draft a will. I did not draw up a list of reasons for or against life, or weigh up facts to make this decision. A decision to kill yourself is seldom conscious. It just happens in a moment when emotions become overwhelming, and, unable to cope with them, you see suicide as the only way out.

I forgot the details—how I opened the window in my apartment, how I stepped onto the window sill, how I decided to jump—but I do remember the voice in my mind saying: "You are ugly, people are disgusted even to look at you, they are afraid of getting your disease, you'd better just stay home so you don't scare anybody, you will never get a job you like, you are not like other people, it's impossible to accept you, you'd better disappear, no one will love you or want to marry you, they will be frightened of having ugly children with you, even you are worried that your children will have to go through what you did. The woman at the florist who gave you a bunch of tulips yesterday only did that to get rid of you, so your face wouldn't scare her clients away. Or, perhaps, she took pity on you. Whatever the reason, it was not to highlight your beauty, as she claimed." Could it be a bad joke, after all? "And the man who entered the elevator this morning? He shuddered in fear. Do you remember how clumsily he tried to explain himself? You frighten people, you should stay away from them, you will never be happy, you'd be better off destroying yourself ..."

... which I tried to do. Fortunately, I failed.

Those thoughts roamed around in my mind, and I couldn't control them. They had settled in long ago, and now they felt like my rightful owners. Sometimes, I managed to contradict them—reject or tame some of them, while grappling with the rest—but I found myself helpless when they attacked me from all around. I knew how to deal with those thoughts one by one, but I could not handle an all-out strike. I knew only how to silence the voices. And I did just that.

———————

It started in school. I was around eight when vitiligo decided to play its tricky game and emerged on my back. I was a big girl. I took showers by myself, so my illness only became evident after it conquered a large enough territory. I still remember when Mama said:

"Come here. What's that spot on your neck?"

She pulled down my T-shirt, peering more closely, and cried out.

We sought medical treatment, but over the next year, vitiligo became part of my self, unjustified but uncompromising. Still, it did not become me. Yet. Back then, I had no idea that in the future the illness would control my life. Sometimes, I even celebrated my "tattoos" and told Mama that my vitiligo had only appeared because she had refused to buy me a Dalmatian. The girls from my class liked me. They looked at the spots with curiosity, and some of them envied me. My appearance gave me some dividends, after all.

———•·•———

Things started up later—on the verge of adolescence, when it finally sank in. The teenage years are a period when you're trying to look nice, to make someone like you, to create your own style. It was then that I questioned the advantages of my condition. Vitiligo was not beautiful—it looked horrible, as if someone had been experimenting with different shades of foundation on my skin. One leg always looked tanned compared to the other, and when the vitiligo climbed up to my head, my dark hair started to turn gray. The girls in my class no longer envied me. Some of them steered clear of me, scared of catching the disease. The changes in my appearance and my status peaked when a new boy joined our class. During the break, when the noise in the classroom exceeded all acceptable levels, the newcomer caught my eye and headed confidently toward me.

"What are you? A frog with white spots?" he asked.

The classroom went silent all at once. Someone dropped a book, someone else froze with a sandwich in their mouth, like in a movie when time stops.

"You're the frog," the girl sitting next to me told the boy, standing up for me.

"Don't call her names!" one of the boys said and kicked the newbie.

Bursting into tears, I dashed to the restroom where I hunkered down until the end of the school day when Mama came and led me away. It was a pivotal moment: I realized that I was not like other people, and there was nothing good about it.

———•·•———

In fact, it all began even later. No one called me names again until I finished school. The locals knew me, and I had long since become used to random strangers glancing at me in the street. But as soon

I stepped into adulthood, all the downsides were there to explore: curious glances gave way to contemptuous stares; interest turned to disgust. People around me, overwhelmed with frustration and self-doubt, raged about themselves and their life circumstances, and I was the perfect target to blow off steam, gloat, or make excuses. "That girl is so ugly." "What happened to her skin?" "I'm happy I don't have it."

"Your hands look horrible," a cashier at the grocery store said.

"You have to do something about it," a woman at the bus stop said.

"No one is ever going to marry you," a man in a train compartment said, unable to keep his thoughts to himself.

Their days get better if they say it out loud. They treat it as small talk about weather, or part of their morning routine. Don't forget to grab a coffee on your way to office—and don't miss your chance to approach that girl sitting at the next table and tell her that her hands look ugly. (You'll blow her mind, she has no idea!) Or maybe one of your friends has a similar condition and you can't help but share such an essential piece of information. If your colleague ruined your day, your lunch was disgusting, your shoes rubbed against your heels, it started pouring all of a sudden, or a car splashed the water all over your coat—don't worry. I, a girl with ugly hands, will appear from around the corner, and you'll regain your good spirits as soon as you remind me about this fact.

Once, a woman at the farmers' market recoiled, looking at me, and said: "I'd rather be in pain than look so ugly."

I just smiled.

She clearly did not understand how it felt when it really hurt.

Vitiligo conquered me. It became my fiercest enemy. Vitiligo became me, so I was my own enemy number one.

Buying clothes that hide all the patches—and not being able to wear that pretty short dress you liked so much. Trying out a million ways of covering up—and feeling as if you are wearing a spacesuit. Devising hundreds of possible answers to all the questions about vitiligo and choosing the right reaction to stares, sniggers, and bullying. Staying alert, responding to jokes with more jokes, keeping quiet in the face of verbal attacks—and dashing to the restroom, like in childhood, sick and tired of explaining that you're alright, it's just your skin, it's just you.

But if you do not stand up for yourself, you will stumble against misunderstandings, rudeness, and accusations again and again. People believe that it is your fault—it is you being careless and neglecting yourself. They consider it their sacred duty to impress that upon you. They only want to help you and set you on the right path. I wish they knew how much their words hurt. But worst of all is that I cannot do anything about it.

———•———

I learned how to live, with varying success. I say "varying" because my mind swirled with never-ending debates and alternating desires to accept myself—or burn myself to ashes. I could never predict which of these two moods would dominate on a given day. I rode a rollercoaster, incapable of finding my balance. As soon as I thought that I'd found an antidote to any attack, people—or I myself—devised new methods of hurting me. And I drowned again.

I was afraid of strangers. At some point, I started to believe in the theory of overpopulation. Going down to the subway, I saw endless lines, rows, columns of people. All of them marched ahead, went up or down the escalator, in and out of train cars, on and on without stopping, always in motion. They frightened me. A perpetual conveyor belt of creatures who are born, grow up, get old, die, replace one another, reproduce, and travel far and wide. They consist of the same ingredients as me, but they are restless simply because my skin is different from theirs.

Strangers became my new trigger. I learned to stand up for myself. I even made friends for the first time in my adult life. But I felt uncomfortable whenever someone new joined our company. I always ended up in the spotlight—and it was due to my disfigurement, to be sure. It seemed to be the only remarkable thing about me. "And now let's all look at Eva. She has vitiligo."

This last sentence is fictional. They never said it out loud but I knew they meant it. "How horrible." "What a shame." I was always ashamed of it, no matter how hard I tried to rewire my brain. The embarrassment gave rise to self-doubt.

"I am Eva. I have vitiligo." This statement took root in me so firmly that I never identified myself otherwise. I could not determine my interests. It was too early to devote myself to one particular career. Vitiligo was my only embodiment. As if it was me. As if I was only that. Vitiligo was the first thing to spring to anyone's mind when they thought about Eva.

I was no longer afraid of questions about my disfigurement. I no longer searched for answers. All I wanted was to stop talking about it. As if it was not there. As if I were normal.

Sometimes, I pretended to be invisible. If I could choose one superpower, I would go for invisibility. Unfortunately, I could do nothing but turn off the light and hide in the darkness. It is a shame you cannot choose a body at birth. I am sure that it will be possible in the future, but for now it's a genetic roulette of biochemical reactions.

The reactions happening in my mind were equally tangled, but, as I said, I learned to live with my illness, with varying success. Frankly, I could not boast of much. But I craved forgetting what brought me to this hospital ward with sloppily whitewashed walls, the smell of rubbing alcohol and homemade food, heavy sighs and the desire to be free again, without knowing, though, what to do with that freedom.

ADAM

Eva's photo exhibition bolstered our spirits—just like her story of becoming a makeup artist. Her success roused us to action. Each of us plucked up the courage to start following our dreams and facing our fears. Too often, the latter are inseparable from the former, and fear is our companion on the road toward happiness.

I remember one Saturday when Anna and I took a stroll in the park. It was a sunny day, and the park was crowded. We sat down in the shade of a tree and talked about unreachable dreams. Anna sighed heavily. It looked like I was the only one that strong, courageous girl exposed her weaknesses to.

I learned her story that day.

"I was born with a hemangioma. That's what that bump on my cheek is called. To put it simply, it's a cluster of extra blood vessels. Usually, they look like a net, but in my case, they tangled up in a ball. A thicket of vessels."

"But you tried some treatments, right?" I asked an obvious question, even though I knew the answer. But it would've been impolite not to ask about it. At least I thought so.

"I had ten surgeries in different countries. Most hemangiomas are removed surgically. But my problem is that a carotid artery runs right through it, so surgery is ruled out. They tried embolization—blocking unnecessary blood vessels. Without blood, they die. But my hemangioma fought hard for her life and always found some ducts to supply blood. My body is just phenomenal."

Her sense of humour always amazed me.

"That's why you didn't have it removed?"

"There is a risk of losing your eyesight or ability to make facial expressions. If I was lucky. The worst-case scenario was they could damage the carotid artery and I would just bleed to death. Nice options, right? So, no, I didn't dare have it removed. Or rather, my parents didn't, because I was too young to decide for myself. And now I'm so used to being like this, I'm not considering any of those options anymore."

"So does it bother you now? I mean it doesn't hurt, does it?"

"No. Things have stabilized. A hemangioma grows along with the body, so after I stopped growing, the problem became less serious. It doesn't hurt, but the organs in my head are constantly in danger. At the same time, doctors don't expect it to get any worse now that I'm a grownup. It was more fun when I was little."

"What do you mean?"

"My hemangioma was unpredictable. Once I had a strong bout of meningitis, and spinal fluid was running out of my nose. Don't even ask me. No one could explain why. If it hadn't run out, it would've got into my brain, and I would've fallen into a coma."

And then she said, laughing, when she saw my face: "Don't worry. My body is truly phenomenal, I told you. But it's a thing of the past. Right now, I'm bothered by hundreds of other concerns. For example, hunger in Africa."

Anna changed the subject, and we talked for a while about global problems beyond our control. It occurred to me that my tic had never threatened my health as much.

"You are very beautiful," I said at some point, filling a silent gap between us. I did not know what pushed me to compliment her. It just came out of my mouth.

Anna was confused.

"You know, compliments always caught me off guard even more than insults. I braced myself for verbal attacks, so I could stand up for myself. But I had no idea how to react when someone complimented me. Those were totally normal things, but they always took me aback."

"When did you realize that you were different?" I said, keeping the conversation open.

"It was a while ago. My first story. That's what I call the turning points in my life—my 'stories.' It happened quite early. I was only nine back then, and I didn't understand much. I couldn't help but notice a bump on my cheek, and it was weird that my friends didn't have it. But that fact never really bothered me. I was more bothered by the need to go to the doctor all the time instead of seeing my friends. After one particularly long absence, a girl asked me how long those travels of mine would continue. Until they take my bump off, I explained, and she said that it wouldn't stop her from being friends with me. Not everyone was ready to be friends with me, though.

"The story I mentioned happened after my next visit to the doctor. My parents and I were travelling home after the checkup. The three of us took our seats on the train. My mother was poring over the papers from the hospital. Father was staring out the window, and I was dozing off to the monotonous chugging of the train. Until another passenger came into our compartment. She said a polite hello, but I immediately disliked her sweet perfume, bright lipstick, and unpleasant, high-pitched voice. The second she plopped down on her bunk, she started making a scene.

"'Oh god. What's that? Is it contagious?! What was the conductor thinking?' the woman yelled in that voice of hers.

"It was all about me, of course.

"The woman wailed that she would not travel in a compartment with a sick child. She demanded that the train be stopped so we could be forced off, even though our papers confirmed that my illness was not contagious. She complained to the train manager. She knocked on the neighbouring compartments to warn the other passengers that there was a monster travelling next to them. Mama yelled at her, Dad tried to calm her down, but she kept yelling accusations at my parents until a crowd gathered outside our compartment. I was sitting with my eyes closed, wishing it would stop.

"Finally, the police arrived, and everyone fell silent. The woman was moved to another compartment. The conductor offered her apologies. The rest of the way, Mama was crying, and Dad tried to reassure me. I couldn't understand what it was all about, but that was when I shaped my first attitude. It is not my problem. The problem exists, alright, but for me it is not a problem. And if it bothers someone else, it is not my job to fix it."

Anna fell silent. We walked for some time without talking. She had to get over the story she had just told—and relived.

"Now you know everything," she said finally.

I nodded.

"And what about Marta?" I asked.

"Marta has a different story."

"Of course. Like any of us."

"Not really," she said. "How long have you been like that?"

"As long as I remember."

"There you go. Marta had to come to terms with the fact that her life would never be the same again."

Marta.

What did I know about her? We didn't see each other much. She was often the first to leave the apartment early in the morning, while the rest of us were still sleeping, and she returned late, tiptoeing around the place so she wouldn't wake us up. She could stay locked up in her room for days, reading what I thought was poetry out loud, sometimes in foreign languages. Italian was her favourite. Marta enjoyed lounging in the bathtub, but only after she'd checked that no one else needed to use the bathroom. She often cooked for all of us—we'd come home after work and find dinner waiting for us on the table. She liked to do the dishes, too, saying it calmed her down. Marta was a perfect flat mate. She excelled at all our in-house activities, but I barely knew anything about her.

When we got together at home or meeting up with social groups, Marta was never a big talker. I did not dare question her, and she never volunteered to talk about herself. That was how it worked: you had to wait until someone initiated the conversation. So, I had to make do with my own assumptions based on her habits and preferences.

Headscarves. It was the most remarkable about her. If someone asked me to describe Marta with only one word, that's precisely the one I would choose: "headscarves." Marta's love for them. Her closet was stuffed with them. She had more headscarves of all colours and patterns than any other clothes. She seemed to change them three times a day. Maybe making headscarves was her small business. "Marta Headscarves," that's how I listed her name in my contact list.

But soon I learned that it was something else entirely. Quite unexpectedly, Marta invited us ... to a play she was starring in. It came as a surprise only to me, though, because Anna had known about it all along, and my astonishment made her laugh. Marta was the lead actress, and during the performance, I asked Anna a few times if it was really Marta I was seeing. She was a completely different person on stage—energized, enthusiastic, and inspired. Whenever I talked to her later, I often caught myself wondering which of the two Martas was genuine and which one was playing a role. But I could never tell. On stage, Marta was bright and happy. At home, she hunkered down in her room. It was only then I realized she hadn't been reciting poetry, but practicing her lines behind closed doors.

At some point, Marta opened up to me. That night, we were waiting outside the theatre to walk her home. But Marta was so excited that she invited us in and introduced us to her actor friends. She gave us a tour behind the scenes, bragging about her new roles, critical reviews, and the upcoming tour. She was so lively, overflowing with energy. When almost everyone had left, she started to pack up her things. And then, locking eyes with me (I was obviously the only one who was still in the dark), Marta took off her headscarf in my presence for the very first time. I saw that she had no hair.

"You have cancer?" I said, after a silent pause.

"Oh no, thank god!" Marta said, smiling, and put on her coat.

MARTA

I WALKED AROUND the building three times, but I still couldn't make myself go inside. Then I made another couple of rounds, hurrying past the entrance as if I was heading elsewhere. I watched the passers-by and the trams arriving at the stop, picking up passengers and moving on. I went into grocery stores and stood in long lines to buy things I did not need. I went outside but still couldn't make myself go into that building. I simply did not want to.

It was hard for me to accept the fact that I needed to buy a wig. The whole process frightened me: I was supposed to find a store that sold wigs, try a few of them on, hesitate to pick one of them, finally decide—and admit to myself that it was not a prop for another theatre role that I could take off after the performance, but a permanent accessory that would change my life forever.

I first noticed it in some rear-angle footage the cameraman recorded at some point in my TV show. I thought it was a glitch. But then I rewound the video a couple of times, and I saw the same image over and over: a bald patch, small as a coin, on the back of my head. I closed my eyes, feeling the shiver running down my spine. I raised my hand and touched the patch, too scared to walk up to the mirror.

I'd noticed that my hair had been falling out lately. But I blamed it on stress, overwork, and lack of sleep, and I was sure that vitamins and hair lotions would fix the problem. Instead, it got even worse.

I am glad to have a habit of going to the doctor whenever I have a concern, even if it's nothing urgent. I developed it after my grandpa died from lung cancer. He had been coughing for a year, but he was only taken to the hospital when he got shortness of breath, even though his family insisted on having him checked out as soon as the first symptoms appeared. The doctor said that grandpa could have been saved if we'd taken him to the hospital in time, if he hadn't been so stubborn. I remembered her words very well. My gyno was annoyed to see me in his office every three months. He assured me that once a year was more than enough.

I was diagnosed with alopecia, and then the doctor rattled off the list of medical terms I didn't understand, like autoimmune thyroiditis. I said that I was not about to look them up on the internet and just asked if that was something treatable. The doctor did not confirm it, but she promised to do her best to help me.

———·———

Alopecia bothered me not as illness per se, but as a condition that transformed my daily routine. I thought about my theatre performances, TV shows, and other projects where I was supposed to change roles—and my hairstyle—frequently. I was a presenter on the morning news and performed at the local theatre. My career had just started to gain momentum, and I had no idea what to expect next.

Meanwhile, I was undergoing a course of treatment—or, rather, a course of experiments, as I called it. I tried typical beauty routines first. The cosmetologist applied all kinds of cremes to my hair, but the foci of alopecia did not vanish. If a bald patch regrew hair, alopecia made an appearance elsewhere. For a while, I managed to style my hair in a way that covered it up, but serious measures were necessary. I took vitamins, continued with my beauty treatments, and then started Kenalog injections. The drug was injected right into the bald spots, and it took me a few days to recover from splitting headaches and general discomfort. I felt uncomfortable at work, too, anxious that my colleagues—or even worse, the viewers—would notice my illness.

"Have you seen that the morning news anchor is going bald?"

"What happened to her? Is that a bald patch?!"

"I think I saw that news anchor in the street yesterday. That one, you know…"

"The bald one?"

The treatment did not help. I asked for second and third opinions, but none of the doctors could tell me the exact reason or guarantee that it would get any better. They promised to do their best. One of them recommended getting pregnant. I was physically exhausted of injections and emotionally devastated. The treatment proved ineffective, so at some point, I stopped it and allowed events to take their course. It was time to look for ways to hide my bald patches.

———•·•———

At first, I wanted to leave television, as my morning show ran the highest risk of potential discovery. Even if I managed to cover the bald spots, my hair was still too thin and ugly.

"Fashion week starts tonight. Our anchor will be there to choose a wig." I felt like saying it on camera and then unveiling some real shock content.

"Is anything wrong?" the producer asked me after one show where I looked insecure and annoyed. It was weird how much my appearance influenced my mood, or the other way round.

"If you need to take a holiday or anything, just let me know."

Looking up at him, I shook my head and burst out crying. It was the first time I cried. The tears spilled out of my eyes, too many of them welled up inside me. I was not a weeper. I hid my vulnerability from my loved ones so they would not get upset.

"Is anything wrong? Do you need any help?" the producer asked, eager to fix the problem then and there.

I pulled myself together. Then I let my hair down. He came closer and looked at it.

"You can always wear a headscarf," he said, refusing to let me go.

His suggestion was brilliant, really. How come it had never occurred to me? From then on, I took to wearing all kinds of head-gear: headscarves, beanies, hats. I liked the way I looked, and it became my new style.

"Why are you wearing headscarves all the time?" someone would ask.

"That's my style."

That answer usually put an end to their questions.

I felt a certain relief after I came out to my loved ones about my illness. That's how it always worked; if others accepted the source of your apprehension, coping with it became easier.

Once, our theatre company went on tour to another town.

"Marta, why are you wearing a headscarf all the time?" an actress asked me.

"That's my …" I cut my usual response short. "I have problems with my hair. I don't want to scare you," I said, confiding in her. Her unperturbed reaction boosted my confidence. After a glowing performance the following night, I decided to come out to the whole troupe.

"This should not be a problem," the director said, trying to reassure me. "But please find a way to cover it up." He meant wearing a wig.

My life got back to normal for a few months, but the situation worsened after the summer arrived. The alopecia was still there. I stopped treatment a few months before, keeping only vitamins. The illness did not progress, but it didn't go away, either. The geography of my bald patches changed. The hair remained just as thin. The air warmed up, and I felt too hot in a hat or headscarf. Having to hide my hair made me weary.

I looked at the people in a crowded subway car; none of the passengers was wearing a beanie, a hat, a cap, or a headscarf. Women had short haircuts or ponytails. Men brandished their tresses, had their hair shaped with gel, or wore dreads. I developed a phobia of bald men. I was the only one in a hat.

I felt as if everyone was staring at me.

"Is she a weirdo?"

"Why is she wearing a hat in summer?"

A hundred pairs of eyes gawked at me and my hat, trying to peek under it. A hundred pairs of lips could not wait to gossip about me. All of them knew what was wrong with me. They stared at me with derision, mocking me to make me feel uneasy. Why did that guy over there keep touching his hair? Why was that lady twirling hers?

What would happen if they saw the real me?

Would the whole subway car explode into laughter? Would everyone call me names? Would they be disgusted to even look at me?

I was losing my mind.

I only looked in the mirror to double-check that my headscarf covered up all the bald patches. A quick glance—that was enough. Never looking into my own eyes. I did not want to see myself, touch myself, or have anyone else touch my hair. Hairdressers were out of the question—I asked my sister to cut my hair. I often hunkered down in my room for days at a time. I took a holiday leave. Then I quit television altogether. Theatre was more comfortable. Depression engulfed me, but I kept on living, riding the wave, trusting it to bring me wherever. I did not feel like making any decisions.

In the end, I got a wig. Too embarrassed to buy it at the store, I emailed a charity organization that collected hair donations to make wigs for children with cancer. I described my situation and said that I could pay for a wig. The fitting was all fuzzy—I just answered their questions mechanically: the preferred colour, the length, the style. The wig was ready in a month. They sent it to me as a gift, and I felt bad about taking it away from some child with cancer. But the feeling passed. I had too many other concerns to torment me.

I could fix the problem physically, by hiding it, and my life was soon driven by this need. It was incredible; only recently, my mind had been occupied with theatre, dreams of being a movie star, and hunting for auditions, but now everything revolved around the mission of hiding my bald patches. To some extent, that too was a kind of art. My external problems could be hidden, but my inner confidence was lost forever. No matter how hard I disguised my appearance, I was always left alone with myself, ruminating about my illness and remembering my life as it used to be. I desperately searched for other remedies, and before I knew it, the night would fall, and it would turn out that alopecia was the only thing that had occupied my mind all day long.

I grew weary of being tied to those headscarves, caps, and hats, of searching for matching outfits and mirrors to check that nothing would give me away. Controlling my movements, hiding from people, staying alert at group photo shoots. I hated browsing through my old photographs where my hair was so long and lush.

I stopped going to auditions. My dreams of the big screen were shelved. Even the thought of being asked to show my hair paralyzed me. Coming in a wig made no sense—the truth would have surfaced sooner or later. A wig was not the best option, anyway. I felt too hot wearing it and struggled with persistent headaches.

At one of the auditions, back when my alopecia was not that apparent and I was still hoping that it would disappear, a fellow actress competing for the same role came up to me and asked if I could take off my headscarf. I politely refused, explaining that it helped me get into character. She was not discouraged, though.

"But still, Marta, could you take off your headscarf, please?" she asked me, again and again. "I would love to see how you wear your hair."

"Are you dumb or what?" I cut her off when she approached me for the sixth time. I was not going to justify myself saying it was my style or I had not washed my hair. "I said I won't do it."

She finally backed off. But I suspected that she'd heard about my problem, as her words were full of sneering. After the audition, she pestered me again:

"So, would you show me your new hairstyle, after all?"

I just left without hugging her goodbye—I was afraid that she'd pull my headscarf off.

Another time, a friend of mine offered to do a photo shoot for me, with a vivid red wig to brighten me up. When she'd finally persuaded me, she found a photographer and rented a studio. For the next two hours, I returned to my past self, energetic and fun—a self-assured actress who loved the camera and was confident in public. I put on my favourite music and laughed a lot, striking different poses. I even drank a little wine. The photographer was satisfied, saying that it was his best photo shoot in some time. He praised me for being so natural, and then he asked:

"Let's do another photo shoot. This time without a wig."

My mood dropped. I sighed.

Oh yes, I thought. I wished for nothing more than going back to the life without a wig.

ADAM

AFTER THAT walk in the park, Marta and I became closer. She spent more time outside her room, but she was still cautious striking up a conversation—perhaps for fear of being a nuisance. Marta kept changing her headscarves just as often, but she was no longer embarrassed to take them off in front of us. They were too tight, she said. Marta and I often improvised, rehearsing parts of her plays, and she predicted a big future for me in the movie industry. I only smiled. The improv fascinated me so much that I almost forgot about my tic, which made my life easier. Marta's life, however, posed new challenges for her. She had to find another job now that she'd quit her television career. Theatre alone could not pay her bills. Marta refused to consider any opportunities for actors, but a mundane job would have destroyed her. She applied for jobs in radio, but with no success. Marta also admitted that she'd started having problems with her boyfriend—or, rather, problems with telling him about her condition. She had been hiding her alopecia for as long as possible, and now she was afraid that it might ruin her relationship.

"I'm surprised that he doesn't suspect anything. Well, then again, he never notices when I change my look—typical guy," Marta said, joking, though she was far from jolly.

Meanwhile, my own life was picking up its pace. Most importantly, I finally started to like it.

I had arrived at a good point in my life. I was more open and less frightened of talking to people, and my tic attacks subsided. David, our therapy group leader, said he'd start giving me assignments. I looked forward to that. Anna tried to involve me in social activities, too.

"We'll be handing out meals to the homeless this Thursday. Are you coming with me?"

"What will I do?" I asked.

"Pour soup into bowls and give it to people. You can also smile and wish them a nice day, if you feel like it."

"Are you sure it's a good idea?"

"Absolutely. What could go wrong?"

"I might get too nervous and spill the soup. Or I could come across as unfriendly. Can I maybe just stand there this first time?"

Anna smiled and shook her head. It meant she was not taking no for an answer.

I had another coming out ahead of me. I was afraid to try something for the first time, especially in public. My therapy group often went bowling together. Those outings were among the assignments David gave us to help us adapt to society. They stressed me out, as I never knew how I would manage. I had never touched a bowling ball in my life, so I had no way of knowing if I'd be good at it. First couple of times, I just watched the others play, saying that I was not into bowling. But that was fear in disguise; I was simply afraid of making myself a laughingstock. I could do anything in public as long as I was confident in my skills, but I kept my distance when facing something new. It was a manifestation of my deepest fear—making a mistake, at work or in any other activity, in anything at all. Making a mistake equaled being a mistake. I just had to be good, if not perfect, at everything I did.

I confided in Anna, and she understood me. That Thursday, I stood next to her watching her give out meals to homeless people. Next time, I tried pouring soup into bowls. Another week—and I fully participated in the process. I felt confident and calm. Happy, too.

"I can relate to your fears, you know," Anna said. "One of the assignments David gave me is to sing in public. I can do a small gig or just sing a song in the street. Singing has been my great love ever since I was a little girl. I've been performing on stage as long as I can remember. Of course, it was back in school where everyone knew me and would not dare to insult me. Later, I gave it up. I never considered singing as a career, but it remained a hobby of mine. And now it's my assignment."

"Are you going to do it?"

"Sure. I'm just waiting for the right moment. I'm curious myself about how it will go. It's not just a personal challenge—it's also a kind of a social experiment."

She paused and then added dreamily:

"Just imagine: a young woman like me comes up on stage. She starts singing. Hundreds of people are sitting in the audience. How many of them listen to her song trying to make sense of the lyrics? Most people are only trying to guess her story: Who is she? Why is she like that? What kind of life does she live? Does she have any relatives? Is she in love with anyone? How often do others turn away from her? Every person is fantasizing about her story. They all feel different kinds of emotion. Some people feel sorry for her, others are raging. Someone else decides it's a joke or stands up and storms out of the room in disgust. I would be curious to watch their reaction. They would stare at me like they're at a gallery but really they're the ones who are the exhibit, and I'll be studying their reaction and sneering at them."

"I've always been amazed at your sense of humour."

"It's my saviour. I love having a good laugh. People often tell me they've never heard anyone talk about their pain and problems with so much irony. I can laugh at myself, too, but that right is mine alone. Nobody else is allowed to do it," Anna said, smiling.

"You like people?" I asked, making it sound as a statement.

"I like helping those who need it. But that's a whole other category of people. Their lives make them accept you just the way you are, because they know they're not perfect, either. No everyone is like that."

She sighed.

"Can you guess how many times I've asked myself if I am an extrovert or an introvert? I have always believed I am this second type. Being on my own felt comfortable. Even in the company of people I knew, I tried to make myself invisible and not attract their attention. I usually held back my opinion, especially if it differed from what most people thought. It felt safer that way. I was afraid that my disfigurement would be used as an argument against me. But then I started doing charity work and discovered that I was more of an extrovert. I enjoy talking to people."

"How did you get there?"

"Charity, you mean?" Anna asked. "Well, I always wanted to organize events, ideally in showbiz—concerts, parties, things like that. But agencies turned me down. Someone even joked that I was only fit to organize Halloween parties. But one day, I saw people waiting in line for food. I talked to the volunteers, and things snowballed. They need my help, and I feel like I belong there."

It was a shame, but many places made people like Anna and me feel as if we didn't belong. One evening, after the last homeless man was given his meal, we decided to get a coffee at a neighbourhood cafe. Anna loved coffee. It seemed to help her open up—it was over coffee that our most intimate conversations unfolded. We went inside.

"Beautiful design," Anna said, looking around, as we sat down at the table.

"I guess it's self-service here," I said. Ten minutes passed, but none of the waiters came up to us.

"It's not," Anna said. Waiters were running around, all busy.

"Sorry, can I get a menu?" I called out, trying to catch a waitress, but she ignored me. Other visitors noticed us alright, though. A young couple came in. They took off their jackets and sat down at the table next to ours, but looking at us, they exchanged glances, stood up, and headed for the door. By that time, a menu had been placed on their table.

"Sorry!" I called out again, but when I rose to my feet to go up to the bar, Anna stopped me.

"Don't," she said, her voice sad. "Let's just drop it."

She clearly did not want to make a fuss.

"They don't want to serve us," she said and stood up to leave. "Let's forgive them."

ANNA

THE SECOND story destroyed my previous attitude. By the way, more than a decade passed between the two of them. Over those years, I faced insults of all sorts, misunderstandings, and rejections. I was annoyed by unwanted sympathy, but then my deepest fear came true—I bumped up against my first limitations. I had blocked out the thought that my disfigurement might somehow prevent me from living my life to the fullest. I imagined it bright and eventful. But unfortunately, I was forced to adapt.

I come from a small town—so small that all its residents know each other. And in the rare case that one of them is not familiar with another, this accident is quickly fixed. My point is that everyone in town knew about my hemangioma, even if they had never seen me in person and they didn't care. But then I left home for college. An established university; intelligent young people—I never experienced prejudice. Strangers in the street pestered me sometimes, but I maintained my attitude and sharpened my sense of irony. Once I'd graduated from the university, I started to look for a job, and it was my entry into adulthood that opened up society's playbook to me.

None of the thirty companies I applied to invited me to an interview. It was weird. The theory of probability was apparently broken. I suspected the reason but stubbornly refused to accept the reality—I hated to think that my hemangioma might turn out to be an obstacle for me. Here I was, an ambitious girl monitoring job search websites all day long, keeping a file with the names of companies where she applied, hunting down new opportunities, and devising new strategies. The most obvious strategy turned out to be the most effective one: the following week, I emailed resumes without my photo. And lo and behold, half of the companies got back to me. Several of them even invited me to an interview.

If I had had more free time, I would have shot a documentary video. With a spy camera, I would have recorded the employers' reactions when they saw me. It was a shame that professional ethics did not allow them to speak their minds. Every interview followed a set routine. They asked me the typical questions, ignoring my disfigurement, even though I was sure it was the only thing that occupied their minds.

"Do you enjoy working as part of a team? What kind of professional literature do you read? Where do you see yourself in a year? Please describe your greatest success."

I nearly dozed off while they rushed through their questionnaires. Why did they do it? Why not just ask me straight: "What's wrong with you?"

They never called me back. Some companies emailed me a form rejection letter, at best. But it tormented me the most because I was struggling to understand whether they had rejected me due to my disfigurement or if it was my professional skills that proved a poor fit for them.

The next two interviews provided exhaustive answers to my questions.

They took place at the advertising agency where I applied for the position of public relations manager. The office administrator greeted me with caution, double-checking if I had really come for a job interview. I nodded. She gave me a quick tour around the office. Chaos was the only thing that caught my attention. Then she ushered me into a cramped glass-walled room in the corner, and, offering a glass of water, asked me to wait.

Soon the director, the head of the marketing department, and another prospective colleague of mine entered the room one by one. They couldn't hide their surprise. Quickly pulling themselves together, though, they took their places in front of me and introduced themselves. That time, I took a different tack. I explained my situation before any of them had a chance to ask me anything. They pretended to understand me, and the director even assured me that it wouldn't impact the professional assessment.

"Oh god! What happened to you?" the HR manager cried out. She had just entered the room.

I had to explain my situation once again.

"Shall we close the window so it doesn't get worse?" She clearly did not understand me.

"Are you planning to hire her?" she said, turning to the director. "Seriously?"

She referred to me in the third person as if I weren't there. The room fell quiet. The men looked at one another. The HR manager obviously had nothing to add.

"Let's stop the interview," I said. "I don't want to waste your time."

The director shook his head and tried to apologize for his employee.

"But she will be a PR manager. She'll have to organize events and talk to media," the woman said, ranting on.

"We'll consider that," the director said, trying to handle the situation.

"We can stop now," I repeated.

"But …" The woman cut herself short this time.

The job interview continued. They thanked me for coming. I thanked them for the water. They never followed up.

At most interviews, I was never asked about my disfigurement, but I found it hard to answer job-related questions with that elephant in the room. The feelings were always there. Amazement. Confusion. Hostility. The question was if the interviewers were polite enough to hold back their comments.

At yet another interview, the manager made careful enquiries about my hemangioma: "Is it temporary? Will you have to undergo treatment?" Then he asked me about my work experience and moved on to talk about his company only to pause and ask: "Are you sure that can't be fixed?" "Sorry," he said, and carried on talking.

Up to a point, it was a pleasant interview with not-so-pleasant conclusions. The manager seemed to treat my situation with understanding, but I knew I would not get the job.

"What is it all about, anyway?" the manager asked suddenly, pulling me out of my reverie. The emotions that filled him up during our conversation finally spilled over. "What's wrong with you? Can you tell me, please? I just can't hire you. No. You'd walk around the office like that, and I would have no clue what's it's all about."

Do you remember my initial attitude? The attitude of denial. Well, at that moment, it crumbled. There is always a trigger capable of destroying all your beliefs in an instant. There are always new challenges you are not ready for, new situations you are not yet immune to. After the series of job interviews, I realized that my hemangioma was a genuine problem, no matter how hard I tried to escape it.

There was my problem. There was my world. There was me.

And the three of us had to co-exist. The state of denial gradually gave way to a state of understanding—a system for accepting myself and my new reality.

ADAM

It took me a while to get over the incident at the coffee shop, but Anna remained unperturbed.

"Good always comes back to you," she said.

I found it hard to accept the fact that it had happened right after we fed a hundred homeless people.

That week, the therapy group discussed how to behave if someone insulted you. I tried to listen to other people's stories, but I just couldn't get my mind off the incident. One could react to insults in different ways, from hitting back to ignoring them. But I decided that in the situations where I wouldn't be able to predict or control my immediate reaction, I'd simply let it go. That way I would not allow emotions to affect me later—even after long fights and self-compromises.

That rule was hard to follow. Sometimes, it took me a long while to overcome stress. At one point, I even started smoking weed. It helped a lot, but it came with its side effects, as the emotional balance I achieved after a few puffs was followed by exacerbation of my anxiety. So, I did not run wild and tried to get by with safer sedatives like music and meditation. After all, it was all about switching my mind off.

Meanwhile, David distributed our first assignments. They were supposed to help us cope with our struggles. It was not a competition, and he did not set any deadlines, but his tasks were supposed to transform our lives, spicing them up. David held them off until he knew us well and could tailor the assignments to our needs. I was afraid of people and their reactions and opinions, so David asked me to surround myself with people in the coming month. My first assignment was to find and pursue a new hobby.

I fell into a trance—I never suspected that so many activities could spur my curiosity. I looked up different hobbies online, then I checked out clubs and societies available in my neighbourhood, and in the end, I tried to remember my childhood dreams and interests. This is what I accomplished in just one month:

Mastering sign language.

When I was little, my father was watching the news on TV when I noticed a lady waving her hands around in a small square in the corner of the screen.

"What's she doing?" I asked.

"It's a language for the people who can't hear," my father said. "Those gestures are her way of repeating what the host says."

"Cool," I thought. "It could be a universal language!"

Now I could introduce myself in sign language.

Getting trained in first aid.

I had been planning to acquire those skills ever since that night at the bus stop when a man collapsed on the ground and I just stood there, with no idea what to do. Ever since, I was haunted by the fear that it would happen to a friend or relative, and I wouldn't be able to help them. Now I felt much more confident.

Learning the rules of soccer.

I always loved soccer, but I was quite sure that the referee was the key figure on the soccer field.

I also joined a community group that got together late at night to look at the stars through a telescope. I learned to adjust a telescope and find the most famous constellations. I tried my hand at pottery, completed a photography master class, and bought a guitar.

David encouraged me to play it—music can calm you down, he said. He recommended taking singing lessons, too. I went go-karting twice, shrugging off the risk. Driving was not my thing but the very fact of it being off-limits made me upset, so I just had to break that rule. The lessons went well, but I did not warm to it. I could easily go hiking now that I knew how to put up a tent, and yoga became my morning ritual, even though I had only planned to take a few group classes. I took up painting again and discovered my love for collecting stamps. The list went on.

But what was I trying to say? I continued to discover and explore new things. When he was giving me that assignment, David explained that it would create conditions that would make me communicate with people. And this, in turn, would help me overcome my fear. I was not sure if it was his original intention, but David helped me understand so much. I realized that the world was fascinating and diverse, and people could be friendly and kind. I never experienced any prejudice against my tic, not even once. I talked about my condition sometimes, of course. What's more, when I really got into something, I forgot about my tics, and they reduced. My assignment, though, was not about Tourette's syndrome. Ever since, I promised myself to take all that the world had to offer. I resolved to travel widely and stay open to all the opportunities that emerged along the way. But it had nothing to do with my task—it was my personal decision, driven by my personal desire.

In search of new adventures, I was also handling the second assignment David gave me.

"You must express your opinion," he said. "It would be great if you did it at one of your classes."

Sounds easy, right? It is quite natural to share your reflections: discuss a movie with your colleagues at the office or talk to your sports club mates about a nice café that just opened in your neighbourhood. It's just as natural to strike up philosophical conversations with fellow passengers in a train compartment. These 'conversations' are merely voicing your opinions to people who attach no importance to your words, as they are just waiting for their turn to speak.

Speaking with others was an ordeal to me. I usually tried to avoid attention and chose the role of a listener, even if my mind swirled with ideas I was desperate to say out loud. It happened for the first time when I was still in school. Our class was supposed to read a short story for the literature lesson, and the teacher asked me to retell it. I stood in front of the blackboard, speechless. Fear swept over me, and the tic started. Dozens of eyes were staring at me, but I couldn't get out a word—I burst out crying and dashed out of the classroom. The teacher settled the situation by promising that, from now on, it would be up to me to decide when to speak in class. I volunteered only when I felt well-prepared and confident because I had practiced my speech at home.

The problem was that I focused on my tics too much. While I tried to imagine how others saw me, my thoughts scattered, and I ended up blabbering a mush of random, senseless words. For this reason, I never enrolled in any competitions and struggled to make a meaningful comment on anything I was not familiar with—or even talk to strangers. I needed time to get used to people; it was only then that I felt comfortable enough to communicate with them.

It became a thing of the past. And I never felt nostalgic about it. I did not realize it immediately, but I completed my second assignment without even thinking about it. When David gave it to me, I had already become so engrossed in exploring the world that I boldly initiated conversations with others, eager to learn new things. I smiled to myself. My world was changing—and I was changing along with it. I enjoyed being the director of my own life and going beyond my limits.

———•◦•———

Marta's situation was more complicated. Marta found it hard to pull herself together and start a new life. Flashes of optimism quickly turned into bouts of depression and days spent behind the locked doors of her room. During her dark spells, she barely ate anything or talked to anyone. I had no clue where she got the energy to go to rehearsals. At first, I tried to help her, but then I abandoned my attempts. It looked like a typical process of struggle. You had to fall all the way to the bottom, feel sorry for yourself, and engage in self-destructive behaviour, only to understand that deep down you wanted to fight and rectify the situation. I underwent that process many times. But for Marta, the situation looked dire.

She contacted radio stations, applying for host jobs. She and I even sat down together and drew up a list of all the stations we knew. Marta emailed them first, and then made follow-up calls. She even visited a few radio stations in person, but none of them was looking for a radio host. There were no jobs for Marta.

"You can apply as a news reporter," she was told at one of the stations. "We might have an opening later." But Marta declined the offer.

After two weeks of fruitless searching, she took to her room, feeling helpless. Whenever she came out of it to have a word with Anna or me, she blamed herself for being incompetent and useless.

"Maybe I should have got myself a real job, like my parents told me. I should've become an accountant or a lawyer. Those people are always sought-after. They have no problems finding a job. But actresses? Who needs them? Theatre is just entertainment. Do you think it's too late now, Adam?"

"I think you should simply be patient," I said.

"Just imagine: things would have been totally different. I would've worked at a bank with a good salary and a clear plan for my future. And what do I have now?"

"Can you really see yourself sitting at the computer from nine to five, crunching numbers? Come on!" Anna said, joining the conversation.

"You're right. Art will last forever. Even in hundreds of years, people will watch the movies I starred in," Marta said, dreaming out loud. Those dreams revived her spirits.

"You can work at my tailoring studio, if you want," Anna said, bringing her back to reality. "Until you find what you really want, that is," she added, trying to soften her suggestion. Marta's spirits sank. She thanked Anna for her support and went back to her room.

"Things will change when her savings dry up," Anna said.

Marta shut her boyfriend out, too. He had no idea what was happening.

"He will leave me if I come out to him about my alopecia. He will fall out of love with me. Why would you have a girlfriend without hair? He'll be embarrassed to be with me around his friends. Disgusted to touch me."

She came up with countless explanations, producing them in a particular order—a new one each day. Marta told her boyfriend that she'd lost her job on television and was taking a pause to cope with the stress. He also invented all sorts of different reasons why Marta wanted to break up with him.

A romantic wave washed over me, too, but it was not triggered by the arrival of spring or a surge of hormones. It didn't resemble what you usually see in movies or novels, either. It was simply another of David's assignments. Yes. It sounded like this: I was supposed to invite a girl on a date. I thought it was a joke, but David was not a big joker, so I only nodded and tried to figure out how to go about it.

I'd had some relationships in the past, indeed, but those people knew me long enough—and they knew everything about me. I put all my cards on the table, so I did not have to explain anything. I even had a couple of one-night stands—admirers of exotic characters. But I could not remember the last time I went on a date. Even the smallest setback complicated the process, let alone my disorder that always provoked too many questions.

"Just choose any girl you like, and that would be it," Marta said. She suddenly perked up, hearing about my assignment.

"Choose?" I said. "What do you mean by 'choose'? The last time I 'chose' someone was my school prom. Girls outnumbered boys in my class, so I had the privilege of choosing my dance partner."

But the assignment sounded wrong to me. As if I was expected to open a catalogue and choose a girl fitting some obscure criteria.

I could not fully understand what David wanted from me that time. How did he envision that "date"?

Did he expect that I would sincerely like the girl? Or was I supposed to go on a date with literally anyone, just to complete the task? Was I expected to date her or try to seduce her? Did we have to flirt or kiss to make it count? What if it failed?

"He just wants you to step into your fear, approach someone and say 'I like you,' and have a walk in the park. Easy. No need for deep reflections."

"I don't think it's a good idea to go up to a girl in a café or in the street all of a sudden. How would you react to that?"

"Well, I always liked it when a guy made a move on me," Marta said, flashing a wide smile. She was clearly walking down memory lane to her amorous adventures.

"Right. Stupid me."

"Don't you have any romantic stories?"

"I do," I said. "One of them happened in high school. A new girl joined our class. She flirted with me too boldly. She shared lunch with me and offered to help with my homework. In short, she was always there for me."

"And what happened next?"

"Nothing. I didn't like her. But it turned out that I'd given her the wrong impression. Can you guess how?"

"Tell me."

"My tic. She thought I was always winking at her."

"Hmm." Marta was clearly lost for words. "Maye you should try that method again. No, seriously, don't dream up anything grand. Go into a bookstore, wait until you see a girl you like, and ask her to recommend a book for you. Or maybe it could be someone who works there. Or go to the concert. I can help you pick a good one.

Or grab some canvas and paints and pretend you're a painter, sneaking glances at the beauties walking by.

"And when you go on a date, try to be confident and make eye contact. Give compliments, but don't praise obvious things—watch out for details. Listen to the girl attentively and ask questions. Then she will believe that you find her company interesting. Before saying goodbye, tell her how much you enjoyed the evening. Then she wouldn't worry if it was really enjoyable."

Then Marta, as a true actress, described several scripts for my potential dates. "Are theatre people always in love?" I wondered. I did not listen to Marta's recommendations, but in a week David's assignment was completed. I went on a date with a girl from my yoga class, the one I most often paired with. After the class, I asked her if she'd mind having lunch with me. She didn't. We talked about all kinds of things and laughed a lot. The date did not follow any of the scripts Marta described—or any familiar script, for that matter. But it was the best date in my life.

I always believed that Tourette's syndrome would hit my personal life the hardest, so I rarely gave much thought to it. It was as if that part of life did not exist and had to be replaced by movies or other hobbies. In the box next to "Marital status," I imagined writing: "A music lover obsessed with movies where dramatic events are played out on such a scale that he doesn't need them in real life. Has the society not reached universal acceptance yet?"

At some point, I felt like experimenting with all known forms of love, trying them all: homosexuality, polyamory, sologamy, fictitious marriage, adopting an abandoned child. But it never went further than that. I could not consider it seriously just like I found it hard to imagine anyone seriously considering me a marriage prospect.

I could register someone's first impression, but I could not read their mind and figure out what the phrase "I accept you as you are" was hiding. What if it served as a disguise for doubts and questions like:

"Is he really a reasonable person?"

"Is it safe to be around him?"

"Will his condition worsen?"

"Can my children inherit it?"

The last question was possible only if the person found comforting answers to the countless previous ones. I would ask questions, too, if I stumbled against something unfamiliar, so my situation looked hopeless. But not dire.

Once, Anna told me about a guy who flirted with her for a while. They met at the university, and she found his attention weird, as he was very popular. She tried to avoid him, doubting that his behaviour was sincere. But as far as I understood, Anna liked him, too. Finally, she yielded to his advances.

"And?" I asked.

"That was the end of it," she said.

"?"

"It turned out that he'd made a bet with his buddies that he'd have an affair with the scarecrow ... me. He admitted it right after we kissed, then laughed at me."

"What an asshole."

"I know. And it was my first kiss ever. Not the best experience, but it taught me a lot."

"But surely you had some better ones?" I said.

"I hung out on dating websites for a while. There were some nice conversations, but nothing more. I only had a date with one guy. He was in a wheelchair, so it seemed like a perfect match. We weren't hung up on each other's issues. But it didn't work out. We were just too different. So, I broke up with him."

"Perhaps you should've given him another chance," I said. That story saddened me as much as the previous one.

"Adam, the fact that both of us had a problem in common did not mean that we were supposed to stay together," Anna said, smiling. She did not seem upset about that.

"My greatest fear was to find myself all alone in it," Eva said at the following group meeting. We were talking about our fears. "I was afraid that people would stop caring about my problems. I felt some relief sharing them with my loved ones, but it played a trick on me later. If you keep talking about one and the same thing over and over, your relatives and friends can no longer find the words of sympathy. They know your story too well. What's worse, they get used to it and lose interest in your problems. And without their support, you're left all alone in your struggle. Most of all, I feared that no one would be there for me in my darkest moments."

Her confession made me wonder, because I never found myself all alone with Tourette's syndrome. I should probably confront it, though, to sort out our relationship. My father often devalued me. Whenever I offered to help him with repairing his car or packing his fishing gear, he didn't let me, saying that I would mess it up. There was hardly a thing I could do without his permission. Mama was even worse—she just did everything for me. My parents were trying to protect me, but they clearly did not realize that it would turn out badly—I would be incapable of making my own decisions as an adult. They used my tic to justify their actions, but later on— let me come clean with you—I rejected quite a few ideas of my own, too, hiding behind Tourette's syndrome.

Meanwhile, our group members continued to share their fears. Someone was frightened of rejection, others worried about health complications. Some fears sounded funny. For example, Marta avoided travelling by plane because she did not want to pull her headscarf down at the passport control area and show the symptoms of her illness in public. I listened to their stories and found a part of myself in each of them. They were like chapters in one long story—only some details and set pieces differed.

I often imagined another Adam—a guy I wanted to be; a guy without Tourette's syndrome, living his life to the fullest without fear of nervous tics. In my fantasies, the tic was simply one of my identities. I asked my "second self" to leave my body and he assumed a human form so I could speak to him. It was a meeting of two enemies who had grown tired of relentless war but had yet to call a truce. Over the years, they got to know each other so well that they forgot the reason for their hostility. I imagined that meeting as a stroll in a springtime park. We sauntered side by side, looking at one another now and again.

"Why do you torture me? Does it give you pleasure?" It would be the first question I'd ask.

"You should pay less attention to me. I don't cause you as much inconvenience as you imagine."

"That's easy for you to say. Why did you choose my body instead of all the others?"

"Believe me—everyone's fighting their own battle. Yours is not the hardest. You have to accept it."

"Is it a punishment or, perhaps, a challenge that I will be rewarded for?"

"It's just a given, and you must come to terms with it. Don't attach too much significance to it."

"My life would have been so much easier without you."

"I do not limit your life in any way."

"If not for you …"

"Then what?" he asked, cutting me short. "Don't forget that I am always with you and I know you well. Come on, admit it; it's just convenient to use me to justify your setbacks, right? I know you inside and out.

"You wanted to study economics, remember? But your father called you a failure and insisted that you work at his factory. And you were afraid of him. Your mother backed him, saying that you could just go on with your life, and she and Father would help you. You agreed to that, because you did not want to argue. It was convenient, too. It was you who did not stand up for yourself. Not me.

"And remember how that real estate agency wanted to hire you? You could have earned money selling properties. They ignored your tic and said they were ready to give you a chance. It was only the result that mattered. But you told yourself that you wouldn't make it. People would not take you seriously because of your tic. You didn't even try. So don't tell anyone that you were rejected. You rejected their offer yourself. You were scared. It was just your fear talking, not me.

"And that blonde girl from the university that you fancied? Remember her? She assured you that your tic did not bother her at all. She wanted to hear your story and give you a chance, but you decided that it would be a problem for her. It's you who decided that, not her. Remember?"

"Alright, alright. That's enough," I said. I did not want to listen to him anymore.

"Of course, you'd interrupt me. You hate to hear the truth. But I'm wondering what you would have done if you didn't have a nervous tic."

"I wouldn't have been scared."

"Are you sure? You would've found countless other justifications, believe me."

"Like what?"

"Like your big ears. Aren't they a good enough reason to think that no one will love you? And you get sweaty palms when you're nervous. You'd feel uncomfortable shaking hands with potential clients, right? And then ... you're boring, Adam. Are you aware of that? You are a dull person. Painting is your only interest. You sit in front of the computer day and night. There's nothing more to your life than that."

"It's not true!" I said, losing my temper. "Well, it used to be true, but now it has nothing do with me!"

"Oh really? What happened?"

"I found new friends. We share a flat. I took up pottery and yoga, and I learned lots of new things, like sign language."

"Really, Adam?"

"I did! And it looks like I've got a girlfriend. I met her at a yoga class."

"Well, congrats. That sounds fascinating."

"It *is* fascinating, goddamn it!"

"Then I've got a question. How exactly did I interfere in your life, my friend?"

My greatest fear was to give up. To surrender. To yield to pressure, lose control, drive myself into depression, start hating or rejecting myself. To feel sorry for myself, go with the flow, find myself in freefall. The varieties of self-destruction are legion.

Living with a disorder is a constant struggle—primarily, with yourself. It is like a computer game where you overcome all kinds of obstacles only to level up and face yet another unfamiliar situation you are not ready for.

I engage in a struggle each time I leave my apartment. People always see me. No, not like this. People always stare at me. They notice my tic and just can't take their eyes off me. Every single day—that's how often I come across people seeing me for the first time.

Imagine walking in the street and having almost every passer-by give you a once-over. Most probably, you will check if there is anything wrong with your hair or your clothes. But I know why they gape at me. And I know how much energy it takes me to fight it. I do some soul-searching, trying to analyze if I have enough of it, and then I argue with myself whether this struggle is worth it. This emotional cocktail gives me a harsh hangover. It takes me a while to recover and calm down. The nervous tic is part of my life, and I don't have any other.

I remember when Marta gave in to weakness and started to complain about her life again. Anna could not bear it and said: "You have to keep looking and keep knocking. Sooner or later, someone will notice you. You'll find a tribe that will accept you as you are. If you're beautiful, people might be jealous of your beauty. If you're rich, you might never know whether someone is actually being sincere with you. Some people will always find reasons to dislike you, but others will need you. And one last thing. Please do come out to your boyfriend. Don't make decisions for him. Tell him—and you will hear an answer. It's your assumptions that are tormenting you, not reality."

ANNA

STORY NUMBER three.

I never wanted to fight with the world. Just as I never wanted to suffer, feel sorry for myself, or let insults bother me too much. Some people stand up for themselves; others get frustrated and depressed. I cherish my sense of humour. A person's attitude to life is genetically determined, I guess. I ignored most incidents and tried to live to the fullest, but I had to accept the fact that I'd have to deal with those who loved putting labels on people.

An invitation to participate in a TV show only confirmed it. The show told the stories of people who were ashamed of their bodies. The idea behind it was to provoke sympathy and show the life of "monsters," the wretched and despicable. I knew, though, that people on the other side of the screen would most probably gloat or sneer. The show's top ratings justified its tear-jerking format. It was not produced to facilitate inclusion or solve the real-life problems of people with disorders. They were merely exploited as fascinating exhibits.

"You must cry a lot, right?" the producer said when I first came into the studio to discuss the script.

"Not really."

"Do people insult you often?"

"Erm …"

"I feel for you. It must be really hard. Please know that we're on your side, and we support you. Let's start the show with a situation when someone insulted you. And then we can talk about your embarrassment. How does that sound?" she asked, flashing a fake smile.

I stood speechless for a moment or two, but then I burst out laughing in her face and hurried out of the studio.

I wanted to appear on TV to demonstrate that I was not ashamed of my body and that people like me were entitled to a fulfilling life. But after I realized that they would edit the show to fit their script, I ignored their calls and messages.

I'd learned to talk about my hemangioma, but I did not have to prove anything. I had no obligation to assure anyone that I was healthy and safe for society or that I had tried all possible treatments, felt anxious and curious, or craved connection and love—and deserved it, too. I was determined to do whatever I liked and help those who weren't so lucky.

I came to the realization that I would have to create a world of my own—just like anyone else with or without a disorder or challenge, as each of us differs inside if not outside. I would have to consider various questions when building my world. I would have to learn to control my emotions and determine my attitude to them, limit the impact of uncomfortable situations, find my tribe and my vocation, and mould myself into a shape I could love. This last task would take the greatest effort.

These conclusions followed from my suffering, insecurity, despair, and escape. But without those things, they would not be so powerful. I had to live through all that to arrive at this point.

I would like you to understand: a body does not equal a person. The picture you visualize when thinking about someone you know hardly matches their identity. Outfit or appearance characterize us only partly. It is our words, our behaviour, our choices that matter. The body is merely rented out to us, with no alternative available. For that reason, I am committed to advocating for people discriminated on the basis of their looks. For as long as I live.

Having realized that, I transformed my life.

Later, I found a job to pay my bills. I also organize events, just like I wanted. I joined a charity: we feed the homeless twice a week, collect donated clothes and toys donations for children in orphanages, and help people with disabilities. And that's much cooler than organizing concerts.

I also signed up for a therapy group for people with disorders. I feel at home in the company of others like me—and this feeling is incredible.

ADAM

IT ALL starts with a decision. You can only take the first step on the road when you have chosen your route. Love for yourself is also a road that you sometimes walk in the dark. It occurred to me recently that it is impossible—and pointless—to avoid obstacles or turn back. We might ruminate about things we cannot change or do not want to accept, but in that case, we'll be walking around in circles. That is the worst thing you can do.

Instead of analyzing your problems or thinking hard how to avoid them, you must tackle them head-on. Otherwise, they will engulf you.

I wasted too much time imagining how my life would look like without Tourette's syndrome. Rather than accept the situation the way it was, I set boundaries for myself and searched for reasons and explanations why it was me who had to live with it. I should have focused on the here and now, instead, and proceeded from there whenever I made new decisions. Too many times, I let my disorder stop me. It was an emotional rollercoaster with endless highs and lows. In those moments, I promised myself again and again that I would change.

That change finally happened thanks to the therapy group, the support I got from others, and my own deep volition. Struggling for a different life, I made a milestone decision—simply to go ahead and try. And it turned out not that bad. But I succeeded only after I wished it with all my heart.

Too often, the biggest obstacle is yourself. And the art of accepting, understanding, and loving yourself is the hardest to master. But is love for yourself not the best therapy?

EVA

MY REHABILITATION lasted six months. Then the doctor said with a smile that our sessions had come to an end, and I had completely recovered and could live an active, happy life. I smiled back—an ironic, melancholic smile. The irony concerned the second part of his conclusion. The melancholy was there because I was not ready for the farewell. I had become used to my new reality: to fellow patients, hospital wards, and even bland dietetic meals. I felt comfortable and unwilling to explore (and get used to) unknown routines. But my mother made sure that things would go smoothly.

The sessions with the physiatrist gave way to the sessions with the therapist, twice a week. I did not feel like seeing her at all, but I tried to conceal my skepticism for the sake of mother.

The therapist's office was minimally furnished in pastel colours and decorated with some plants with names I did not know. The sofa I was lying on was quite comfortable. Ruining this bliss was a woman with a notepad and a pen who was asking me a series of pre-prepared questions in her melodious voice. She strictly followed the protocol—I had no doubt about that.

The first three sessions were disastrous. The therapist was apparently trying to get to know me, so I had to retell my story down to the smallest detail. Anger, self-pity, misanthropy—I was triggered to feel them all. "She's just pushing my buttons. What a great way to help a patient," I thought. She blabbered about how much it mattered to let yourself vent, untangle the knots inhibiting your movements, work through your childhood traumas and the psychological barriers you've set up in adult life, and other nonsense. Wearing a carefully ironed dress, with immaculate makeup and a perfect figure, she was droning on, making me drowsy—and ready to murder her to stop her monotone voice.

I couldn't bear it any longer.

"Listen," I said. "This bullshit might work for some crazy ladies who are bored of living in comfort and are searching for some mystical sense—or nonsense. Whatever. I have a real problem—vitiligo. But I can see that it does not really fit your profile."

Finishing my little speech, I burst out laughing. Then I calmed down and fell back on the sofa. The therapist listened to my arguments politely and pretended that they did not offend her. She continued to ask questions in her measured voice. I sighed heavily and resorted to sarcasm.

"No, I don't see much meaning in life."

"Yes, I will make new suicide attempts. No, jumping out the window is too banal. Perhaps I will set myself on fire. Will you help me with that? Or at least film the scene on your phone?"

"Or now that I think about it … I'd love to try saving turtles that wash up on Australian beaches or travel to California and practice Zen meditation. Or find another kind of 'zen'. It's legal there. I can share some with you. Would you accept that as payment for this session?"

I have no idea what she thought about my answers or whether she could tell when I was joking and when I was just teasing her. There wasn't much that was serious about our sessions. But I had to complete the course, so I decided to go along, after all. I felt sorry for her, and even more for my mother. I wouldn't get much use out of these sessions, but at least I would make them happy.

"What do you want your life to look like?" the therapist asked me at the beginning of our next session.

Her question confused me, and I started to look for a catch. But then I decided to give her a polite and honest answer. The conversation had not started with inquiries about my vitiligo, so it deserved a chance.

"It would be great to start my mornings with workouts. I'd like to be a freelancer and have a flexible schedule, working with people I like. I would also like to read a lot, learn French, and travel around France."

"Do you have any childhood dreams you'd like to act on?"

"I'd love to dance. I have always dreamed about performing on stage but somehow it didn't pan out. When I was little, Mama signed me up for music lessons instead. And later, I just couldn't make time for dancing classes. But I must do it one day."

"How do you imagine your relationships with friends?"

"I would love to throw house parties. Friendly and warm, you know, Yulia?" I said, calling her by her first name. I hardly noticed when I switched to this informal manner, but for some reason I thought it was proper. "Board games, chill music or light comedy on the background, tasty snacks, laughter."

I smiled. Then I smiled again, this time at her, as if apologizing for my being rude to her earlier. And once more, at myself. My potential life fascinated me.

An hour-long session flew by. I was disappointed when the administrator knocked on the door, warning us that our time was up and another client was waiting. I shook Yulia's hand and smiled again. Apparently, she had drawn certain conclusions from my previous visits. I liked it much better when we simply talked, and she was not trying to "fix" me.

Our conversations about my vitiligo unfolded in a different key after that. Instead of stirring up negative experiences, the therapist helped me recall positive moments.

"Has anyone complimented you on your peculiarity?"

I stalled. Memories reeled in my mind—childish jealousy of other girls in school, teenage compliments from boys that I found pleasing. But the warmest memory went back to one of the darkest days in my life when I had my appendix removed. I told Yulia how

I was lying on the operating table, and the surgeon, looking me over, said: "Oh, I see you're a special one. Beautiful, like a leopard." My face melted into a smile, as I was slowly losing consciousness—either from his words or from anesthesia finally kicking in. That moment was a turning point for me.

Yulia smiled. It was quite unexpected, as she always tried to observe professional ethics.

"Has there ever been a real chance to cure your vitiligo?" she asked.

"Not really. Once I managed to consult a renowned dermatologist, but his verdict was disheartening. I'm grateful to him for being honest, though. It helped me consider my problem from a different angle. But I am not sure something that cannot be solved is a 'problem.' He said that vitiligo was merely a cosmetic blemish, and I couldn't do anything about it. He also recommended staying away from the experimental medicine that I favoured back then. In his opinion, it was only damaging my health."

After that visit, I finally exhaled. You might regret not doing something that you could do. But when the umpteenth attempt fails, you feel as if you have a moral right to step back. Letting go of regrets and worries is sometimes the best decision. My emotions and actions progressed from self-pity to searching for reasons to looking at the bright side of things. But it was only after hearing that I did not need to fight with my vitiligo that I found my peace. I could confront people who tried to hurt me, but the most intense struggle was the one raging inside me.

"Have you ever tried to change anything about yourself?" Yulia asked. Our session continued.

That moment, I started to believe in psychotherapy. I felt grateful for Yulia's patience, too.

She asked the right questions, in the right order—only when I was ready to give answers that could help me.

Yes. I tried to change myself. Only once. Vitiligo lightened my hair, turning it into blondish-gray. The colour looked uneven and ugly, but it was one thing I could change.

When the hairdresser turned me around to look in the mirror, the reflection showed a stranger. "Who's that?" I asked, bursting into tears. I hated the brunette I saw.

The hairdresser suggested trying different shades, and the manager offered a partial refund. But they did not understand that I was crying because I was angry with myself—for refusing to accept myself for so long. The woman I saw in the mirror was not me. It turned out that I liked myself the way I was.

"What do you want to be?" Yulia asked and closed her notepad. It meant that our session was almost over.

"I'd like to become a makeup artist and make people beautiful," I said, smiling confidently.

"And how does vitiligo stop you from becoming one?"

It was our last session. The following week, Yulia was moving to a new town, but she promised to come visit one day and invite me for dinner as her friend.

"Do you have any recommendations for me?" I asked.

"Allow yourself to go for a beach holiday. And try to look at other people as much as possible."

The light breeze on the beach carried the fragrance of the salty sea. Noon was still far away, the sun was gentle, and the sand warmed my bare feet. Wrapped in a long dress, a shawl around my shoulders and neck, I strolled along the waterfront, recalling the last couple of days. I bought three scoops of my favourite lemon ice-cream, then sat reading a book for a while. It grew hotter, and I splashed my feet in shallow water, thinking that a trip to the seaside had been one of my biggest dreams, one that I hadn't allowed myself to make happen. Following Yulia's recommendation, I looked around and saw a remarkable picture: hardly anyone had a picture-perfect appearance. Some people were overweight, others skinny; some of them limped, others had moles or burn marks, scars or scoliosis. I saw bald heads and hairy shoulders, large bellies and unshaven legs. And all those people were allowing themselves to enjoy the sun and the sea.

A few minutes of observation made me reconsider my illness. Hiding, feeling embarrassed, not letting myself live to the fullest—all of it was my own choice. It also occurred to me that the appearance issues of those other holidaymakers did not bother me in the least.

The fear of rejection had overwhelmed me. It was not connected with someone in particular. Neither was I fighting to please everybody. But I was afraid that I wouldn't get a job I wanted or an organization I'd applied to would reject me. When I fell in love, I was never the first one to confess my feelings. Being in love meant being vulnerable. As long as the other person had no clue about it, you were safe, at least from being rejected—not because the feelings were not mutual but for looking the way you looked.

However, the situations I feared so much almost never happened. My fears had nothing to do with reality. People could call me names or tease me, but they still accepted me, one way or another. If I did not draw people's attention to my vitiligo, they often did not mention it, either. That lady at the farmers' market told me that she'd choose being in pain rather than looking the way I looked. Later, I reworded what she said: "I am not in pain, so why should I limit myself?"

I was the one who set limitations. I was the one who restricted myself. I was the one who drove myself into emotional abysses. I did not allow myself even to try things that interested me for fear of embarrassing myself. I never signed up for a salsa club because I was afraid that no man would choose me as his partner. I was scared of posting my photos on social media. But when I finally created an account and showed myself to the world, some people sent me supportive messages like "You're doing so well" or "I'm impressed with how you're holding up." At first, I had no idea what to make of their support, but then I decided to prepare a photo exhibition. I had no choice, right?

ADAM

Each of us is fighting our own battle. It comes in many different shapes and forms, and even if it has spared you, it is tormenting one of your friends. Whenever I meet someone for the first time, I feel like I'm opening a new book. I am not familiar with this person's story—just as they are not familiar with mine—but I know for a fact that at that very moment they might well be struggling with something or other. So, I try to be kind to them.

In my whole life, I have never met a single emotionally healthy person. Everyone lugs around their old baggage of childhood traumas, teenage issues, or the daily grind. But I know how delightful it is to win this battle. The secret is quite simple—do not search for happiness or fight for it. We already have all the resources to create our own happiness. It is enough to allow yourself to be happy. But it takes great talent to do it.

That day was special. I was looking forward to it for the entire week. In fact, the whole week was special. I spent it doing things I love. I returned to the office—it felt great to arrive in the morning, drink coffee with colleagues, and discuss work issues or news. They welcomed me, and the tic did not stand in my way. Perhaps they just knew me well enough as their remote team member, or maybe I did not draw too much attention to it. I do yoga twice a week, immersing myself in my self, and that always relaxes me. I've made good progress with my guitar, and sometimes I even jam with friends at home. Mary and I still see each other. She's the girl I met at the yoga class. We still keep some distance, but overall, it feels great to be together.

I am happy alone—I carried this feeling with me to the last meeting of our therapy group. I became a new person, a new Adam who decided to arrive a bit earlier to enjoy the atmosphere for the last time. I went up to the second floor, as usual, and looked out the window, giving me a wonderful view onto a small park and a bookstore nearby. I greeted everyone entering the room. I arrived earlier precisely for this reason—to say hello to every member who'd become so dear to me.

David was the first to speak. He said that he was satisfied with everyone's results and believed that we could achieve all our goals. He was proud of us and loved us. Then David asked the most crucial question in the entire course:

"During our meetings, we've discussed many issues. We talked about how to stand up for ourselves and talk about our disorders properly. We looked our fears in the eye and learned to accept ourselves. But before we say goodbye to each other, I would like us to discuss one last question. What is the thing in your life that you're most grateful for?"

We kept quiet for some time, as if waiting for someone else to volunteer an answer. Or perhaps we were just relishing the moment, grateful to be here and now. It was a pleasant pause.

"I am thankful for my home," Anna said. "Every day, I walk past dozens of homeless people. It's hard to look at them and wonder where and how they will spend the night. Especially when I know that I'll spend it in the comfort of my own home where I've got food and hot water. I'm grateful to have friends, too."

"I am thankful for having my family and friends who help me survive tough times," Eva said. "My skin looks different, and it often gives me a hard time, but I can see, hear, talk, and walk. Many people can't do that. I am grateful for having a chance to live a full life."

We lingered for a while after the meeting. It was a night of warm conversations among people who shared an important part of their lives—people who understood each other perfectly and would stay forever united by one story.

For a long time, I was nostalgic for our meetings. Humans are social creatures, after all. The sessions had come to end, but I still felt support, replaying our conversations. This new, positive trigger took root deep inside me and nourished me long after I left the room that night. We entered a new world. The world we were ready to build. We were full of hope. Full of love.

A year passed. It brought on quite a few changes. It was remarkable how much could change in such a short time. Each of us headed our separate ways, but our lives remained connected.

Eva committed herself to the world of fashion. Having worked as a makeup artist for six months, she opened her own parlour. Her appearance attracted people: it inspired trust somehow, and her business flourished. It boasted some celebrity clientele—famous actresses and singers. Later, Eva discovered another talent and became a fashion designer.

Anna is still involved in charity. Only now she works for a large organization, doing countless events. This fulfilling activity makes her feel needed, she says. I see Anna more often than the others. We meet almost every Thursday at the same old place where she gives food to the homeless, whom she considers her family.

Anna fulfilled her dream, too. She performed on a great stage. Anna's song was the conclusion of a performance at Marta's theatre. The audience gave her a standing ovation. She burst into tears, and I had never felt prouder of her.

Marta stopped playing the assumptions game. At the moment when she thought she'd lost everything, she allowed the world to decide on her destiny.

She came out to her boyfriend about her illness. He asked for some time to think. The next day, he asked her to marry him. Marta is now pregnant. Her hair is slowly growing back. She wants to return to television. For now, she writes scripts for her signature show.

Adam. Me. I continue to explore the world and myself. It is the most fascinating journey, I must confess. Herbology became a new addition to my list of hobbies. My room is now filled with various plants. I love to watch a new life being born. My other interests include history, especially the early modern period. It has fascinated me since my travels around Europe. Reading is a significant part of my life, too. It gives me a chance to discover the life I cannot see with my own eyes.

All in all, I am holding up well.

I am doing alright. Mood swings do happen from time to time, but they're part and parcel of anyone's life. So, when I say "I am doing alright," I really mean it. It's only that the scriptwriter creating the stories of our lives catches me by surprise sometimes. They lead me down roads I never planned to take.

At some point, I stopped looking far into the future and learned to live in the present. Our lives changed and affected us in some way or other, but we just kept living them. Deep down we stayed just as we were: emotional, sincere, childish—the way we'd remain until the end of our days.

IVAN

THIS BOOK came as a surprise even to me. I never planned to make a book out of this story, even though I always wanted to tell it. When writing, I had to remember—and relive—all those unpleasant moments. It has been the hardest book in my life so far—and the most important one, too. I personally know every hero. They are real people. I wrote this book not for myself, but for those who need support and who lost their kind hearts. There is as much truth in it, as there is fiction.

I love looking back. It's my bad habit. Usually, it does not do me any good, but this case is an exception. Tourette's syndrome gave me a lot of grief, but I gained so much. I learned patience and resilience. I stopped judging others and how to tolerate setbacks better. I no longer make demands of others, of the world, of myself. The nervous tic gave me a chance to weed out unwanted people and things and find myself faster. The tic only eased off after I reconciled with myself. It was as if it told me: "You cannot get rid of me, but you can swap me for peace and harmony. So, search for love and fill yourself with it."

This story will never be over. Tourette's syndrome will be my eternal companion wherever I go. I fought with it for too long. What I should have done instead was learn to live with it. All my victories and insights are products of my experience, often bitter and painful.

IN(VISIBLE)

I cannot write "The End." to finish this story, but the book does need to end. I began to write it back in February when it was damp and cold outside. It's April now. Today, I woke up and took a deep breath. Then I took a hot shower and brewed some delicious coffee, welcoming spring, rebirth. I went for a walk. The sun was warming my skin, my favourite music was playing in my headphones. I looked at the people around me, hearing snippets of their conversations and bearing witness to their lives. I made plans for the evening: cook dinner, read for a bit, call my parents. They always say they miss me and ask when I'll come visit them. Today, I smiled a lot. My mood was wonderful. Tourette's syndrome helped me realize the most essential thing. As soon as you start thinking about what you are grateful for, you forget about things you do not have.

Warsaw. February — April, 2020

ACKNOWLEDGEMENTS

The author expresses his gratitude to Natalia K., Oksana M., and Anastasia Kh. for their help with this book.

Thanks to Bogumiła Berdychowska and Yulia Fedorchuk. This book was written during the Gaude Polonia residency.

Special thanks to Len, Natalie, Micki, family and friends for their support in getting this book translated into English.

About the Author

Ivan Baidak (born in 1990) is a daring Ukrainian fiction writer whose debut novel *Personally Me Personally for You* (2013) became a national bestseller and garnered excellent critical reviews. His two short story collections, *Role Plays* (2014) and *The Shadows of Our Dates* (2017), topped bookstore bestseller lists. His latest novel *A Man With My Name* (2019) was excellent proof of the writer's maturity.

2020 saw the publication of his most recent novel, *(In)visible*, which received publicity among the elite of society. The book was recognized as one of the best books of 2020 according to PEN Ukraine. A play and several photo exhibitions were staged based on the book.

Originally from Ukraine, he's lived in many places across the world, including Poland, Austria, Mexico, and the United States. His short stories have been translated into English, German, Serbian, Polish, Spanish, and Italian, and presented at European literary festivals. In 2019, the author's debut Euro-tour took place, during which Ivan visited Warsaw, Krakow, Wroclaw, Prague, Berlin, Munich and Paris. He received a scholarship from Gaude Polonia 2020.

Since leaving Lviv in February 2022, he was hosted by Camargo Foundation in Cassis, France, and Slovenian Writers Association in Bled, Slovenia. He plans to make his way to Canada in September 2022.

About the Translators

Hanna Leliv lives in Lviv, Ukraine, where she works as a freelance translator and runs literary translation workshops at the Ukrainian Catholic University. She was a Fulbright fellow at the University of Iowa's Literary Translation MFA program and a mentee at the Emerging Translators Mentorship Program run by the UK National Center for Writing. Her translations of contemporary Ukrainian literature into English have appeared in *Asymptote*, *BOMB*, *Washington Square Review*, *The Adirondack Review*, *The Puritan*, and elsewhere. In 2022, *Stalking the Atomic City: Life Among the Decadent and the Depraved of Chornobyl*, a non-fiction book by Markiyan Kamysh, was published in her translation by Astra House.

Isaac Stackhouse Wheeler is a poet and translator from New Hampshire, best known for his work with co-translator Reilly Costigan-Humes on English renderings of novels by great contemporary Ukrainian author Serhiy Zhadan, including *Voroshilovgrad*, published by Deep Vellum, and *The Orphanage,* published by Yale University Press. Wheeler's poetry has appeared in numerous journals, including the Big Windows Review, the Peacock Journal, and Sonic Boom. He holds an MA in Russian Translation from Columbia University and is currently earning another in English Secondary Education at CCNY. Wheeler's first poetry collection, *The Eleusinian Mysteries*, is available from Aubade Publishing.

Printed in August 2022
by Gauvin Press,
Gatineau, Québec